Coffee and Crushes at the Cat Café

Coffee and Crushes at the Cat Café

a Furrever Friends Sweet Romance

by Kris Bock

Pig River Press
9781698810232
Copyright 2019 by Christine Eboch

Chapter 1

Kari studied the muscular, tattooed man with the shaved head. Yummy. Not her type, but still, she could see why some women liked bad boys. "You don't look like a barista." Whoops, had she said that out loud?

One corner of his mouth twitched. "You don't look like a business owner."

Fair enough. Growing her hair out had not, as she'd hoped, helped her look older than her 24 years, and no matter how tall she stood, she couldn't reach above five feet two inches. All right, technically five feet one and a half inches.

She smiled. "I guess we're even."

He glanced around the empty room. Kari followed his gaze. Was he wondering if they would actually get the cat café open in a few weeks? At the moment, they had no furniture, no decor, and no cats. This man had wandered in through the doors that were propped open to let the paint fumes escape. He wasn't the first person to take interest in the Help Wanted sign in the window, but he was one of the few men, and the oldest. She guessed his age at early thirties, though possibly hard living had added a few years.

His presence made the large room feels smaller. Kari took refuge in professionalism. After all, however she might look, she was in fact a business owner now. "Do you have a resume?"

He turned back to her and his piercing gaze almost knocked her back a step.

"I'm going to be upfront with you," he said.

She swallowed. "I'd appreciate that."

"My resume doesn't reflect my current interests. I did four years in the Army. Then I signed on with a private security firm in the Mid East. Did that for four years before I was injured last year. Almost two years ago now, I guess."

Kari did some math in her head, partly to distract herself from his golden-brown eyes. Assume he'd entered the military right out of high school. That made four years plus four plus two. That would make him younger than she'd thought, less than thirty. Eight years in the Middle East would also explain his tough, weathered look.

"I spent the time since then focused on healing. Physical therapy, counseling." His eyes narrowed slightly, as if ready to judge her response.

"That's good." It would be rude to ask about his injuries, not to mention against labor laws if this was going to be a job interview. "I hope you're ..." It was probably too much to expect *better* from a recovery that took over a year of physical therapy and counseling. "... improved."

He nodded, and his shoulders dropped half an inch. She hadn't realized until then that he might be nervous about this conversation as well.

Kari smiled warmly. "So now you think making coffee sounds good? Or is it the cats that appeal to you?"

He returned her smile, and her knees went weak. He was not her type. She liked intellectual, career-focused men. She had never understood women who raved over a man in uniform. Not that he was in uniform now. She glanced down at his faded jeans and tried not to let her gaze linger on the snug black T-shirt as she looked up again. Now he looked like he should be jumping on a motorcycle without a helmet, not looking for work in a café that featured adoptable cats. Soldier or biker, he wasn't her type – but she could see the appeal.

A clatter came from the kitchen, where her sister was organizing the supplies. On the other hand, this man might be Marley's type. After all, Marley had gotten pregnant at eighteen from a tattooed soldier on leave. She'd hardly dated since, but if her ex hadn't turned her off of the type permanently, she might find this one appealing. But was he a nice guy or a jerk?

"Both, actually."

It took Kari a moment to realize he was responding to her question about coffee or cats. She needed to focus and not let her thoughts race ahead.

"I tried a lot of things to deal with the PTSD," he said. "Meditation, yoga, even knitting." His eyes narrowed again, as if daring her to laugh.

She glanced at his hands, with the thumbs tucked into his front jeans pockets, and tried to imagine those hands working knitting needles. They'd be strong and rough against the soft yarn. She cleared her throat. "Does anything help?"

"I haven't gotten the hang of meditation yet. Mostly I feel bored. Yoga has been good for rebuilding my strength and balance. Knitting ..." He shrugged. "At first it helped because it was so challenging that I couldn't think of anything else. Now I'm losing interest."

"It sounds like you get bored easily."

"I like to be productive. Making a scarf when you could buy one for less than the cost of yarn doesn't make sense to me."

"Sure." Kari shifted from foot to foot. It felt like they'd been standing there forever, though it couldn't have been more than ten minutes. "Come into my office and sit down."

She waved toward an open doorway, but he waited for her to take the lead. The back of her neck prickled as he followed behind her. She wasn't sure she wanted someone so ... intense ... working for her, but at least he was interesting. She'd give him a chance to tell his story. And maybe introduce him to Marley before he left.

Her office had a desk and a computer, although no Internet yet. Fortunately, they'd already moved in a guest chair so she could interview potential employees. She rounded the desk to her chair and waved him toward the other seat.

"I didn't get your name yet," she said. "I'm Kari."

"Colin."

A lovely name. One that would feel good to say, nice and round in the mouth. She needed to not think about mouths. "You were telling me about how you got interested in coffee and cats."

He leaned back in his chair and studied the large, framed poster of kittens on the side wall. "Who wouldn't like cats? As for coffee, I'm not a connoisseur, but I like a good cup, and I can learn all the fancy stuff." His gaze returned to her. "I started cooking mainly to feed myself. I was getting flabby from too much fast food."

He didn't look flabby now.

A smile softened his lips. "Turns out cooking is fun. Focusing on the colors, the smells, the tastes. That helps keep me in the moment better than meditation. So eventually I got into baking."

Kari sat up a little straighter. "You bake?" They already had a baker: her sister. But Marley couldn't work seven days a week. Plus, this would give Marley and Colin something to talk about. Maybe even something to do together. Marley's son was nine. He was old enough to handle his mother dating, and Marley needed more fun in her life.

Colin liked cats. He did yoga, baked, and knitted. He was open about his need for counseling. Lots of checks on the nice guy list.

Colin leaned forward and said in a seductive voice, "You should try my salted caramel blondies."

Was it getting hot in there? Kari resisted the urge to fan herself. "I'd love to." Goodness, her voice sounded husky too. She cleared her throat. "Were you hoping to do some baking for the café?"

"That would be ideal. I'll do anything though. Make coffee, wait tables, clean bathrooms, mop up hairballs.

Believe me, I've done harder and less pleasant jobs in the military than anything you could come up with here."

Kari glanced at the cat poster and back at him. "Forgive me for saying this, but it seems like you're way overqualified for any job we might have."

His golden eyes danced. "I'll take that as a compliment. I want you to understand where I'm at. That's why I'm being upfront with you."

"Right, your injury." She couldn't see any damage, but a lot of injuries were hidden. "Does it keep you from doing things?" She should've asked if he 'required special accommodations.' But since he brought up his injuries and therapies, he wasn't likely to sue her for asking about it.

"Not so much anymore, but I'd like to reenter the workforce slowly. I don't want too much stress. I like baking. I like animals. I haven't been spending a lot of time around people besides medical professionals. I'd like to be someplace where people are relaxed, happy, having fun."

"I certainly hope Furrever Friends Café will be that way."

He leaned forward, one arm braced on her desk. "I don't mind working early morning shifts, evenings, weekends, whatever. I may need to schedule around some appointments though, and I'd rather start with shorter shifts, no more than six hours."

"I think we could work with that." She couldn't ask about his relationship status in a job interview. Still, it sounded like he didn't have anyone waiting for him at home.

Was she actually considering hiring this guy? He might find the café relaxing, but Kari didn't think she'd find his presence restful. Still, it would be unethical to refuse him employment because she found him attractive and a little intimidating. She hadn't gone to business school and done all the work of starting her own business at age 24 to be a sleazy employer. She'd done that work to make life better for her family, and she wanted to create a great workplace for all their employees.

A burst of singing came from the kitchen.

Kari made a sudden decision and stood. "I'll need to see some ID, do paperwork, run a background check. Training starts next week for baristas and cat care. Right now, come meet my sister Marley. She's our lead baker. I'll let her decide whether you belong in her kitchen."

He stood and waited for her to circle the desk and lead the way out of the room. It was kind of creepy, the way he trailed behind her instead of walking next to her. At the kitchen doorway, she glanced back. Was he limping slightly?

She turned away and pressed her lips together to hide her smile. Funny how her opinion could flip in a matter of seconds with more information. If he was trying to hide a limp, that made him vulnerable instead of slightly threatening, but proud, too, and she didn't want to embarrass him.

Marley came out of the storage room and broke off in the middle of a P!nk song about being a rock star. Her eyes widened and her mouth stayed open as she took in Colin.

Kari snickered. "Hey, Marley, meet Colin. He wants to work with you."

Colin stepped forward and offered a hand. "Pleased to meet you."

Marley snapped her mouth closed as her cheeks flushed pink. "I didn't know anyone else was here." She shook his hand.

"He wandered in off the street," Kari said. "He claims to be a baker. If he can also sing, you two could do duets."

Colin shot her an amused look. "I'm afraid my skills are limited to humming and air guitar, but you sounded great."

Marley's blush deepened. "Thanks. So, baking? This is our kitchen. You could probably tell that."

Marley was so cute when she got flustered, but Kari could give her a minute to collect herself. "We need someone to take the weekend morning shifts, and any days Marley is sick or has a conflict." But that wouldn't get the two of them together. "Marley will be supervising any other bakers we have. Maybe you can set up a time this week to work together and see how it goes."

Marley beamed at Colin. "I'd love a second opinion on my menu. Kari handles all the business, but I'm in charge of the food, and I don't know what I'm doing. We've done research – Kari must have talked to every café owner in the city – but it's hard to judge demand when we haven't even opened yet."

"I've never run a café before," Colin said, "but I'd think you'd want to keep things simple at first. You can always expand the menu later, but keep it easy for yourself as you find your footing. In any case, people will mainly be coming in for the chance to play with cats, right?"

"That's our hope," Marley said. "But I want them to love the food too."

"I'll let you two get acquainted," Kari said. "I have things to do."

Marley looked from Colin to Kari and back again. She wiped her hands on her jeans.

"What were you planning on serving?" Colin asked.

"Right. I have the menu here." Marley swung toward the big table in the middle of the kitchen. "If you have any specialties, we can add them."

Marley pushed a brown curl off her forehead as she leaned over the table. She was taller than Kari, curvier, darker, older, prettier, more talented. More everything. Kari might have been jealous, except life hadn't been fair or easy for her big sister. Kari wasn't even sure what dreams Marley had given up when she got pregnant, because Marley didn't talk about her dreams anymore.

The man who fathered Brian had left town without a backwards glance. Marley lived with their parents, raising her son and waitressing evenings and weekends when someone else could look after Brian.

Well, no longer. Now Marley could work mornings in the café, doing the baking and supervising the early staff. She could finish by two and greet Brian when he came home from school. She could spend weekends with her son. She never had to miss another soccer game or school play.

And if Kari had her way, Marley would find some fun – maybe even some romance – for herself.

Kari had gotten all the opportunities Marley had missed. It was time to pay it forward.

She studied the two of them leaning over the table, discussing the menu. They could be good for each other. Colin's injuries might trigger Marley's nurturing instincts, helping her get past her nerves around his tough masculinity. But he would never allow her to turn into too much of a mother to him. He had a softer side, and he wasn't afraid to show it, but nothing about him was weak or needy. And if he could make Kari's knees wobbly, surely her sister wouldn't be able to resist his sex appeal.

Neither of them glanced up as she slipped out the doorway. Her plan was working. She was good with plans. That twinge she felt wasn't regret, or envy. She didn't need a man who made her feel fluttery or foolish. She still had tons of work to get the café open, and then months more of work and worry to make sure it was a success.

Her personal life could wait.

Chapter 2

He had to get away from the screaming.

Colin liked cats, he really did. Of course he'd wanted to be there when they brought the first cats to the café. Every animal had been checked for health problems by a vet. They'd been vaccinated and fixed. The shelter workers had chosen cats that would get along with each other and with people in the open environment of the main café room. All the cats would be available for adoption, with the hopes that customers would bond with one or more.

The café wouldn't open for a week, but they had the furniture and plenty of cat toys. A smaller, separate room had pet beds and litter boxes. Lots of litter boxes, plus a closet full of bags of litter. Kari and her cohorts at the shelter wanted to give the cats a few days to adjust to the location before interacting with customers. At the same time, the staff could get used to having cats underfoot and fine-tune the guidelines about how often those litter boxes got cleaned.

Welcoming the cats to their new temporary home had sounded fun.

It turned out to be a madhouse.

The day had started well enough. Sure, every staff member had come in for the event, and some had brought friends or family. Colin wasn't used to that many people milling around randomly, but he'd met a few of them, and everyone seemed relaxed and happy as the shelter workers brought in the first animals.

A couple of the cats yowled when in their carriers. Who could blame them? But once they were released, the first cats explored their new home with nervous curiosity. A few were ready to play or cuddle within minutes. Marley's nine-year-old son, Brian, sat cross-legged on the floor, waving a pole with a string, while a gray kitten batted at the feathers attached to the other end. Marley had a big grin as she took pictures. Kari watched them proudly, and when Colin caught her eye, she flashed him a smile that lit up the room.

Then the shelter worker brought in a carrier holding a handsome Siamese called Samson.

Samson yowled like an air raid siren. And he didn't stop.

The shelter worker opened the carrier, but she couldn't coax out the cat. Samson seemed to think he was a prisoner of war. How did you explain to an animal that this was a safe place full of cat toys and cushy beds, where he might meet people to give him his forever home?

The yowling went on and on until Colin thought his head would explode.

Other cats started to get nervous. A few meowed. One had a high-pitched whine. Marley, distracted by the cat chaos, didn't hear the beep of the alarm on her watch telling her to remove the apple tarts from the oven. The fire alarm shrieked.

Colin fled.

He ducked through the nearest door and closed the door behind him. Kari's office. He collapsed into the guest chair, covered his ears with his hands, and hunched over, rocking slightly. At least it was quieter in there with the door closed. He was safe. No one was trying to hurt him.

His heartbeat slowed. His breathing evened. He was going to be all right. The cats would be all right.

The fire alarm ended. The cat's wailing faded more slowly, until finally Colin couldn't hear it any longer.

Behind him, the door opened and closed. He jumped up and twisted to look.

Kari leaned back against the door. "Whew. That was a bit much." She tipped her head to one side. "What are you doing?"

He hadn't realized he'd moved, but somehow he was at the far side of the room, one fist clenched and his other hand grabbing uselessly at empty air where he used to carry a weapon.

She gave him a crooked smile. "Too loud for you? I don't blame you."

He stared at her, unable to answer.

She bit her bottom lip for a second. She didn't look directly at him as she spoke softly. "I took some psychology courses in college. I learned a little about PTSD." Her glance met his and jerked away. "I'm not claiming I'm an expert. Only that I know a few basics, like sudden sounds can trigger flashbacks."

He wouldn't think about the embarrassment of having her see him like this, having her recognize what was happening.

Stay in the moment. Focus on now.

Studying her helped. The sound of her voice, the curve of her cheek, the movement of her lips. Those lips would be soft, and they might taste of the lemon bar he'd seen her sample earlier.

She studied him. "If you need to be alone for a while, just say so."

"Lemon bars."

"Excuse me?"

He chuckled weakly. "Sorry. That's what you remind me of."

"Okay?"

He rubbed his hands over his face. "I know I'm not making sense." He dropped his hands and looked at her. "Marley is more like a blondie. Sweet, tender, but with enough substance to hold up, and lots of interesting little pieces inside. You're more like a lemon bar. More tart than sweet, and you look soft but you have a firm layer underneath."

She wrinkled her nose, like she wasn't sure that was a compliment. But it was. He enjoyed looking at her delicate features, but even more, he enjoyed seeing her tackle all the problems associated with opening a business. She was tough when she had to be, but he'd never seen her be unkind. She had the perfect blend of sweet and tart.

He probably shouldn't try to explain that. Better to change the subject and hope she forgot his stupid comment. "I guess Samson finally settled down."

"Unfortunately, no. They're taking him back to the shelter."

"To kill?" He took two steps toward her without meaning to, his fists clenched again.

She held up her hands, palms toward him. "No, no, not to kill. They'll keep him at the shelter. But this might not be the best fit for him, with too many strange people and other cats."

"All right. Fine. Good." It was only one cat, out of millions in the world. If Samson did get put down, no one would remember him in a week. But Colin had had enough of suffering and death.

Kari shifted nervously, crossed her arms, let them drop, and finally tucked her hands into her pockets. "I never asked, do you have any pets of your own?"

"No. I'd like to, one day."

"One day? Why not now?" She gestured toward the door. "Take your pick."

He shrugged. He wasn't ready to take care of another creature. He had a hard enough time taking care of himself. He hadn't dated since his injury either. First he had to make sure he was safe to be around. He didn't want to hurt a person or a pet during a panic attack or one of his flashback episodes.

He hadn't had a major meltdown in months. He'd thought he was almost better. Almost ready.

Today had proven otherwise. He still had a long way to go.

He didn't want to tell Kari any of this. It was bad enough she'd seen him in this state.

He scowled. She shouldn't have come in after him.

No, that was unfair. It was her office. He should have known better than to escape there. He should've fled the building.

He was breathing too fast. Maybe he wasn't calm yet. And he'd thought this week was going so well.

"I need to get going." He tried to get past her to the door.

She stopped him with a hand on his arm.

"What?" he snapped.

She flinched and pulled her hand away.

"Sorry." He blew out a breath. "I need some fresh air."

"Quick question. When we open, will you be all right in the main room?"

He clenched his jaw. "I'll be fine."

"I was just going to say that we could keep you in the kitchen at first. If it works with your schedule, I'd like you there with Marley every morning until we get a better feel for the workload. You don't have to serve people."

Great, now she thought he couldn't handle a few random café customers and cuddly cats.

And maybe she wasn't entirely wrong.

"Thanks, but ..." He wanted to insist again that he'd be fine. But if he didn't believe it, why should she? "Let's see how it goes." He forced himself to look into her eyes, hoping he wouldn't see pity.

She looked worried. Could be worse.

"I promise I won't ruin your opening," he said.

"Of course not. Marley has really enjoyed having your help in the kitchen. I'm so glad you two are getting along."

He nodded. He enjoyed working with Marley in the kitchen. They'd quickly become friends and felt at ease with each other.

"Marley is amazing," she said. "Don't you think?"

"Yeah. I guess it runs in the family." He shouldn't have said that. She might think he was flirting, and that would be awkward, what with her being his boss, and him being unfit for a relationship.

Not that he hadn't thought about it once or twice. It was fun watching Kari bustle around, triple checking everything, training new employees, and talking with contractors and suppliers. It was even more fun watching men twice her age slowly realize that she wasn't merely a cute young thing, and she wasn't going to be fooled by their promises or put up with their condescension. She marched around taking charge of everything, like a dog marking its territory – but without the urine. He smiled at the thought.

"What are you smiling about?"

He could not tell her he thought of her like a dog, with or without the urine. She hadn't even appreciated being compared to a lemon bar. More proof he wasn't ready to date, if he couldn't come up with a decent compliment for a pretty woman.

"Nothing," he said. "Merely looking forward to next week."

She laughed nervously. "I'm glad one of us is. I'm trying hard not to panic."

He turned toward her and met her gaze directly. Her eyes widened and her lips parted.

He placed his hands on her upper arms and held her gaze, willing her to believe every word he said. "This place is going to be amazing. You've done a fantastic job."

She swallowed, blinked a few times, and finally nodded. "Thank you."

He winked and slipped out of the room before he had too much time to wonder why his heart was suddenly pounding again.

Chapter 3

Kari carried a stack of picture frames and color printouts from her office. Photos of each of the featured cats would hang on the wall, with information about them: their sex, age, and a short personality profile, so potential adopters could learn more about the cats they most enjoyed. Helping cats get adopted wasn't the only reason she'd opened the café, but it was a major bonus.

She'd have more room to spread things out on one of the big tables in the main café. Plus, if she chose her position right, she could spy on Marley and Colin in the kitchen. They had to keep the cats out of the kitchen, so they had a glass door that would allow anyone leaving the kitchen to check for lurking cats. The serving counter had a metal grille that stayed down when they weren't serving, but you could see through the gaps in the wire mesh fairly well. Between those two things, Kari could catch glimpses of Marley and Colin. She could not, unfortunately, overhear all of their conversation.

His behavior the day before had set her on edge. She'd never felt in danger; she simply wished she knew how to help him more. The obvious solution would be to ask, but that hadn't seemed the right move when he was already jumpy and frustrated.

She set her items on a table and inserted the first picture into a frame. A gorgeous black and white cat leapt lightly to the table and sat watching her, its tail twitching. Marley flipped through her pictures until she found one that matched. "Aren't you a handsome boy, Domino. And so well behaved. I'm sure you'll get adopted right away."

In response, Domino walked closer, sat on the pile of photos, and purred.

Kari chuckled and rubbed his head. "Goodness, you like that spot in the middle of the forehead, don't you?

Maybe we should add 'favorite place to be petted' to our descriptions."

If only humans could be so upfront about what they liked. She should find a time when Colin was calm and happy, and initiate a conversation about his PTSD. She had to ensure he'd never harm Marley – or other employees and customers. Kari didn't really think Colin was physically dangerous. He'd mentioned counseling and all the other ways he dealt with anxiety and PTSD. Even when Samson was screaming, Colin had been brusque but not physically out of control, and his instinct had been to retreat rather than attack. Still, better safe than sorry.

As his employer, she had to be careful about asking questions. She'd review the ADA laws for specific rules. Since he had already disclosed his disability, she should be safe asking what accommodations he might need, but if she recalled correctly, she couldn't ask about the extent of his disabilities or whether he was taking medication.

As his employer, it was her right, even her responsibility, to ensure that her employees were suited for their jobs and to give them the support they needed. Maintaining that employer and employee facade might make it easier to have a calm, neutral discussion about practicalities. She excelled at practicalities. Witness how she grabbed an electric, spinning cat toy, showed it to Domino, and set it running on the ground. Soon Domino and several other cats were thoroughly distracted, and Kari could get on with her work.

Marley sang the folk song "She'll Be Coming 'Round the Mountain," and Colin accompanied her by drumming on the counter and adding his rumbling voice to repeating "when she comes."

Was that a rather naughty form of flirting? Knowing her sister, not likely, at least on her side. Marley often sang old folk songs to or with Brian. Kari had heard her sing this one dozens of times before. She'd never noticed the double entendre before hearing the words in Colin's husky voice.

The pair broke into laughter. The sound almost drew Kari into the kitchen. But a third wheel would not help them connect with each other, so Kari would simply stay out of their way and do her own work, by herself.

Kari might be a little lonely, left out of the fun, but that would change once the café opened. Until then, it was often only the three of them in the mornings. Colin and Marley prepared items that could be frozen, then thawed and baked when needed. That would help them keep up with daily demand, without having so many baked items that some wouldn't sell. Kari couldn't bear the thought of wasting food, but if they made too much and then tried to eat everything they didn't sell, they might regret it.

Maybe Marley should be the one to talk to Colin about his issues. That would avoid labor law violations as well as Kari's own discomfort.

No, that could backfire. Marley had such strong nurturing instincts to begin with, and Kari didn't want her sister playing the role of mother instead of potential lover.

Kari slid the last picture into a frame. She had nails, but she needed a hammer to put the pictures on the wall, and she'd forgotten to bring one. She should get a toolbox for the business. In the meantime, the photos could wait until tomorrow.

She sighed. It was time for another round of litter scooping and checking for hairballs anyway.

Colin paused at the glass door, checked for furry marauders, and slipped through to the main room. "Need help with anything?"

Kari grinned. "Good timing. I was about to search for hairballs."

He chuckled. "I'll help. Like I said, you can't gross me out with anything here."

"That sounds like a challenge. Hmm. How about birth? You ever witness one of those?"

"Actually, yes. Not a cat, but I did see a dog give birth, and one memorable time I helped a farmer help a cow deliver a calf. You'll have to try harder."

"We shouldn't be getting any births here anyway, unless the vet really missed something." Kari wrinkled her nose. "Or one of our customers goes into labor."

"That would be a new experience. I always did enjoy new experiences."

They were kind of, sort of, talking about children. His thoughts on human children would be important if he got together with Marley. Not that they had to get married and fill a nursery right away, or ever, but since Marley already had a son, she wouldn't date anyone who didn't like kids.

Kari hesitated a moment before taking the plunge. "Do you like children?" It was definitely a tangent, but not *too* off-topic.

He shrugged. "I guess I feel about kids like I feel about cats and dogs, and adults for that matter. I like some better than others, and I prefer they don't jump on me or lick me." He bobbed his eyebrows up and down. "With the occasional exception, of course."

Kari laughed and tried to ignore the image his joke brought on. "You've met Marley's son, Brian, right? He's a great kid."

"Yeah, he seems cool. No surprise, given his family." Colin looked at the framed pictures of the cats. "Are these ready to go on the wall? I could do that."

"I forgot to bring a hammer."

"I have one in the toolbox in my car, but you're not planning to hammer nails into the wall, are you?"

Kari glanced at the pictures and then at the wall. "What else would I do?"

Colin gave an exaggerated sigh and shook his head. "You would hang them properly. Since you'll be changing the pictures frequently, you want the system to be sturdy so the nails don't pull out of the wall. I'll get some anchors that will stay in place, and bring in my level and stud finder." He looked at her expectantly.

Kari crossed her arms and tried to look prim. "If you're waiting for me to make a joke about already knowing how to find a stud, keep waiting."

Colin saluted as he headed for the door. "I'll be back in half an hour."

Kari called after him. "Don't think I haven't noticed which of us is going to be mopping up hairballs."

The door closed on Colin's laughter. Kari stared after him. That conversation had veered off-topic quickly. At least he seemed to like Brian, and he had made a subtle compliment to Marley with the comment about Brian's family. His flirtatious jokes didn't mean anything. Or maybe they meant he had been flirting with Marley, and the mood spilled over. That would be good.

"Was that laughter I heard?"

Kari turned to see her sister at the other side of the counter, leaning on her elbows. Sweat dotted Marley's forehead from the heat of the kitchen and her cheeks were rosy without the aid of makeup. She looked happy, and Kari's heart swelled.

"I guess you put Colin in a good mood," Kari said.

"One of us did. Come try these cookie dough brownies."

Kari crossed the room. "Did you say cookie dough *and* brownies?"

Marley lifted the metal grille six inches and pushed a plate toward Kari. "A brownie bottom layer with raw cookie dough on top." Smears of chocolate and crumbs showed that the plate had once held more than the current three squares. "No egg in the cookie dough, of course, so it's safe raw."

Kari picked one up and took a bite. She closed her eyes with a murmur of pleasure.

"Tell me about it," Marley said. "It's a good thing I'm on my feet so much or I'd be gaining a pound a day."

Kari finished her third bite before she spoke again. "I suppose eventually we'll get used to all these goodies and they won't be so appealing."

"One can dream. I'm going to set aside these last two for Mom and Brian."

Kari made a little whimper but nodded. "You have more in the freezer?"

"We made a pan of twenty-four, and now we've eaten three ... or maybe five. Who's counting? It's important to taste test." Marley put the remaining cookie dough brownies in a plastic container. "We have ten different items, and we'll put out six or eight options each day. That should let us see what's most popular so we'll know which to replace."

"I'll go on record as betting that these will be popular."

Marley grinned. "Of course we'll keep trying new recipes as well. I'm thinking if we wind up with three or four favorites, we could have those all the time, and the rest will change. We're discussing seasonal options as well."

Kari licked the last bit of cookie dough off her fingers. "Somehow I don't think I'm going to get bored with these treats. And I'm not on my feet in the kitchen all day."

Marley snorted. "I've hardly ever seen you sit still. But once we get things going, maybe we should join a gym or start jogging or something."

"I will if you will." Kari tried to look innocent. "Does this mean you're feeling the urge to look good for someone?"

Marley tossed her head. "Please, I look fantastic for the mother of a nine-year-old boy."

"You look fantastic, period. And you've seemed happy lately. Are you happy?"

Marley leaned over the counter and reached under the grate to put her hand on Kari's arm. "The last few weeks have been so much fun. Instead of delivering food someone else made, I'm actually testing recipes, baking, and creating menus. Learning a little bit about how a business works. Hanging out with cats, and singing in the kitchen, although I might have to stop that when we have customers. Thank you for this."

Kari blinked back tears. "I'm glad we can do this together. It's working all right with Colin?"

"He's a sweetie. Don't let him get away."

Kari frowned. What did that mean? She would certainly keep Colin as an employee if she could, but she could only offer flexible hours, reasonable benefits, and cuddly cats. If he stayed, it would more likely be because of Marley.

A crash came from behind her and she jumped. Kari swung around and searched for the source of the noise. A gray tabby sat on the table with the framed pictures, looking innocent as she washed a paw. It took Kari a moment to notice the picture that had landed on the floor. Domino came up and nosed at it.

Kari marched across the room shaking her head. "Is that any way to behave, little girl?"

The tabby didn't even glance in her direction.

Kari moved Domino off the picture and examined it. "Now I have to glue this frame. It's a good thing we didn't use glass." She checked the name of the pictured cat. "Do you have something in particular against Cleopatra? Or merely something against anything sitting on *your* table?"

The gray tabby looked straight at Kari and meowed.

"Yes, yes, lesson learned." Kari gathered up the rest of the pictures before the tabby, called Misty according to her picture, could do more redecorating. She headed for her office. They couldn't put in a double door there, like they had at the front door, so she had to dodge the cat trying to rub against her ankles, open the door, and step over the cat gate. It wouldn't be a disaster if a cat got into her office, but the goal was to keep cats in the main room where people could visit them. The cats had plenty of hidey-holes if they weren't feeling sociable. If they really wanted to get away, they could go to the smaller back room that held the cat beds, food and water dishes, and litter boxes.

Colin came back moments after she'd finished scooping litter boxes. Still on her knees, she straightened and fisted her hands on her hips. "What, were you watching through the door until you knew I was done?"

"Done with what?" He put on the fakest innocent smile she'd ever seen. "I've been hard at work getting the proper tools for your picture-hanging job."

"Uh huh." She stood and picked up the plastic bag. "I'll just take this bag of used kitty litter to the dumpster while you get the pictures from my office. Don't leave them unattended or Misty might practice voodoo on her enemies."

She turned back at the door. "And I'll have you know, I ate the last cookie dough brownie."

He chuckled. "I know where all the goodies are stashed. *And* I have the recipe."

By the time Kari return to the main room, Colin had arranged the framed photos, a level, a power screwdriver, a tape measure, and some other odds and ends on the table. He had also accumulated an audience of cats. He plucked Misty from the table as she reached a paw toward the level.

By the time he put her down and turned back, Domino was nosing at the pictures.

Kari grabbed the black-and-white cat. "I'm beginning to think we should have gotten all the decor in place before introducing the cats." She found the electronic cat toy and set it running. At least that distracted a few of them.

Colin used the stud finder to identify the best places to hang photos, measured the height, and screwed in picture-hanging doohickeys with the electric screwdriver. Marley joined them and ran cat interference while Kari hung the photos on the hooks and straightened them using the level.

"Looks great," Marley said at last, wiping her hands on her jeans. "I have to run to meet Brian after school. Be good." She dashed for the door.

Colin raised his eyebrows. "Do you think her command was for us or the cats?"

"The cats, I'm sure. At least, *I'm* always good. I can't speak for you."

He leaned closer. "Trust me, I can be very good."

Kari turned away to hide her blush. How did she wind up flirting with him? She wasn't trying to attract him. He simply had a playfulness that made it easy to joke around. No doubt he was that way with Marley as well.

"What are you thinking about?"

"Um." Kari blinked rapidly. She'd been staring in the direction of the photos on the wall, without really seeing them. "Just making sure everything looks even." She almost complimented him on his work, but that might lead to another double entendre.

The flirting didn't mean anything. But now they were alone. The big room seemed smaller and too private.

Domino rubbed against her ankle. Colin and Kari weren't alone. They were surrounded by a eight cats. That should be enough chaperones for anyone.

Time to change the subject to something safe.

Chapter 4

"I keep thinking about Samson," Kari said.

Colin winced. So much for the sexual tension that had filled the room. Reminding him of his meltdown was a good way to shut down his libido. Just as well. He'd been having so much fun, he almost forgot that he was not ready for a relationship, and definitely should not be starting something with his new employer, no matter how cute she was and how much fun it was to tease her.

"I feel bad about my reaction," he said. "I'm sure he's a great cat. I wouldn't be happy being stuck in a little cage and carried across town either."

Kari nodded. "I met him at the shelter and he's an absolute sweetie. One of those big marshmallows. I'm sure he'd be adopted in a flash, if the right person came along. Too bad it won't be here."

"Have you considered adopting him yourself?" Funny, now that he thought of it, neither Marley nor Kari had ever mentioned having cats at home.

"I wish." She bent to pick up Domino and cuddled him in her arms. "My mother is allergic."

"Marley mentioned that the two of you, and Brian, live with your mom."

"It was the cheapest way for me to get through college. Marley stayed because of Brian. It was convenient to have babysitters on hand, and of course it saves her money as well."

Kari rubbed her cheek against Domino's head. "Then Dad died last year. We wouldn't want to leave Mom alone now even if we could. Not that I plan to live there forever, but getting this business going has cost even more than I predicted, so it's hardly the time to increase my expenses."

She shrugged. "Anyway, it's nice to have company when I get home."

Colin grabbed a chair and straddled it, facing the back. "It's great that your family gets along so well. Must be nice for Brian."

"Losing his grandfather was tough for him. For all of us, of course, but now he doesn't have a man in his life." She wrinkled her nose. "I sort of hate that idea, that he needs a man to teach him to be a man. It seems like we should be past that gender stuff. But I worry that he'll have questions and won't want to ask us."

"Nobody has a perfect childhood, but I'll bet Brian has it better than most. He'll manage."

She gave him a look he couldn't interpret. He'd meant to be supportive, but maybe she thought he was diminishing her worries. He hated when people said, "It will be fine," when they had no way of knowing that it would.

He should probably leave. Kari had left it to Colin and Marley to decide how much he should come in that week, and he'd been there a lot. He hadn't been worrying about getting paid, because he had a good insurance settlement from the company he worked for when he got injured.

Still, Kari might worry about paying employees when they weren't even bringing in money yet. Starting a new business had to be expensive, and she was so young. He wanted to ask how she'd gotten the money, but an employee shouldn't question his boss about that kind of thing. Besides, she might think he didn't believe someone her age could manage it, and she already got enough of that attitude, from what he'd seen.

The silence stretched as Kari walked along the line of photos, studying each one. Usually she seemed so focused and full of energy, but occasionally, like now, he sensed loneliness. Did she have a life beyond her work and family? Did she want one?

Those topics were too personal, especially if he was trying to keep his distance. Instead, he said, "So your mom's allergic to cats, and you're opening a cat café. How does that happen?"

She turned with a smile. "I suppose you could say I'm opening a cat café *because* Mom is allergic."

She headed toward the kitchen. "You want some coffee? We have this fancy espresso machine and I haven't been taking advantage of it."

"You want me to make it? I think I figured out most of the coffee menu, though I still have to check the instructions for one or two of the more obscure ones."

"That's all right, I need to practice too. I'm sure I'll wind up working the counter and the floor more often than I'm in the office."

A cat meowed loudly at Colin's feet. He bent to run a hand over its back. "Sorry, no coffee for you. You guys are enough trouble without caffeine."

While she ground beans in the kitchen, he sauntered toward the counter and leaned against it from the café side. Probably good to keep a barrier between them.

"Don't think you're going to distract me with a cappuccino so I forget about your cryptic comment," he said. "Surely you didn't open a cat café because your mother wouldn't be able to visit it."

She flashed a grin. "That would be delightfully diabolical, but no. I've always wanted a cat, and Marley adores every animal. We must've taken Brian to the zoo weekly for the first five years of his life. It's still one of our favorite days out." She tamped ground espresso into the portafilter. "Brian would love a dog or a cat or even a guinea pig, but with Mom's allergies, he's stuck with goldfish."

"Those aren't quite the same."

"Hardly. I wanted to open a business, where I could be in charge, and Marley could work and – well, anyway, I liked the idea of a café."

She poured milk into the steaming pitcher. "There is overhead for the equipment, of course, but the startup costs aren't as much as, say, a clothing store where you need a lot of stock. Most cafés don't make food on the premises. They get it delivered from a bakery or corporate headquarters, so the café doesn't need the licensing and inspections of a restaurant. We could've done the same, but Marley loves to bake, and I wanted our offerings to be unique and amazing."

She gestured to the kitchen behind her. "Plus, we got this place, which used to be a restaurant. The building owner is an elderly cat lover with no heirs, so she gave us a great rent-to-own deal. I learned how to put together a business plan and got a loan from a group that helps small local start-ups."

He waited until the steamer finished hissing before he spoke. "That's impressive. I don't imagine they give many people your age loans."

"Not so impressive. We put Mom on the paperwork as my business partner, and we had life insurance from Dad, so it's not even a huge loan." She pushed a cappuccino across to him.

When had she noticed cappuccino was his standard choice? "Still, you should be proud."

She shrugged and looked away. Not someone comfortable with praise then. Also not someone used to letting other people take care of her, or even used to taking days off to be lazy. He'd be willing to bet her idea of "free time" was helping take care of her nephew.

She needed more fun in her life.

He pushed away the thought. It wasn't his place to help her have fun.

But being a workaholic could have a major downside, he knew from experience. It had seemed smart to sign on with a security company. It wasn't as if he liked the heat and stress and danger of working in the Middle East, but the private company paid well and had great benefits. Five years with them and he'd have money to go back to college, start his own business, or simply travel the world for a few years. It seemed like a no-brainer after doing similar work for the military for a fraction of the reward.

He'd known the dangers to his body and mind. The risk had seemed worth the rewards.

It hadn't been.

She finished foaming milk for her own cappuccino.

"Your mom really won't be able to visit your business?" he asked.

"She started allergy shots. She said there was no point before, because Dad had allergies too and he wouldn't do the shots. He hated needles. Now Mom wants to be part of things here."

"So Brian might get his pet someday."

"I sure hope so, but not for a while. Mom's been doing the shots for a year, and she's seen improvement, but desensitization takes a long time. For now, she's our social media manager, which is a big help, and she can do that from home, after her main job."

"I did wonder why I hadn't met your mother yet."

"You probably will this week. She'll have to keep her visits fairly short, take an antihistamine, and change clothes afterward. Marley and I strip off our clothes as soon as we get home and toss them in the laundry."

He tried not to imagine that.

He sipped his cappuccino. "Nice. You got the foam good and hot."

"I worked at the college café for two years. Not everyone realizes you can foam milk without fully heating it. You need to stick the wand deep in there and let it buzz for a while. That's the only way to get things really hot."

Great, now everything sounded dirty to him. She had to be doing it on purpose. Except she couldn't possibly be doing it on purpose. She was busy wiping down the steamer wand and didn't even send a flirtatious glance his way.

"You didn't explain where the cats come into this," he said.

"Oh, right. Well, the café made business sense. We all love animals. Cafés are becoming a thing, but our town didn't have one yet. It helps us stand out from the other cafés and bakeries, and we get to play with cats, and cats get adopted. The shelter loved the idea. They have connections with vets who do the health checks and spay or neuter, so we don't have to worry about that part. The shelter handles the adoptions, the paperwork and checking that people are suitable. The adoption fees go to the shelter and they pay the vet a discounted rate for the medical stuff."

"Everyone wins."

"I sure hope so."

This attraction had to be all on his side. She probably liked businessmen in suits, guys who had career plans and investments, not damaged almost-thirty baristas. He'd landed in a great place with this job, so he should count his blessings and try to be good friends to both sisters. They were sweet and hard-working and too innocent for someone like him.

If he was a good friend, and only a friend, he'd help them have equally innocent fun after they worked so hard.

She was watching him over the rim of her cup. How long had he been daydreaming? He scrambled for something to say. "I was looking at some other cat cafés online, to see how they did things."

"Oh? How do we measure up?"

"You'll definitely have the best homemade baked goods, and the best-looking employees." He winked. "But it's not a contest. I was merely curious, since it's not a typical Starbucks business model. Some of the cat cafés have events. Photo workshops with the cats, cat painting classes. Yoga, things like that."

"Yes, I know. I'd like to do that eventually, but I'll need to connect with people and figure out the pricing and –" She broke off and shook her head. "It's a little overwhelming right now. Let's just get through this opening."

He sipped his cappuccino. "I know some yoga teachers. When you're ready, I can introduce you. You could probably set up an income share, where you each take a percentage, so you can't lose money. That will also encourage them to recruit their own students to participate."

Her smile warmed the room. "That would be great. When I started planning this, I had so many ideas. They're all in the business plan. But it's been hard to keep up."

"It doesn't all have to happen right away."

"I know. That's why I'm doing this soft launch. I don't want to do much advertising until I make sure we have things under control. I've heard of restaurants that get a bad reputation in their opening weeks, because the staff isn't trained, or the cook doesn't know how to handle a large volume of orders quickly. They improve, but the restaurant can't shake that early reputation. I'm playing it safe."

He didn't want to argue, but opening her own business didn't sound safe to him. With her brains and work ethic, any big company would be lucky to have her. She'd be in management by age thirty. But she wouldn't have the control she wanted, and she wouldn't be able to lift up her family with her.

She wrinkled her nose. "I can't wait too long to bring in money though. I planned so carefully, and even built in some buffer, but it's still been more expensive than I expected." She tossed her head. "Sorry. Not your problem, and I don't mean to be a downer."

She looked left and right, as if checking to make sure they were truly alone, and leaned closer. "Would Marley notice if I snuck another one of those cookie dough brownies out of the freezer?"

He leaned in and whispered back. "Check the fridge. There's a container of rocky road fudge bars that broke when we tried to get them out of the pan. We'll blame their disappearance on a cat burglar."

She grinned and headed toward the fridge.

She was trying to keep her whole family happy, and the stress was weighing on her. Nothing he could say would really help. But maybe he could do something. He knew what it was like to have life overwhelm you. He was finally coming up for air after a year-plus of physical therapy and counseling. It had seemed like he spent every minute exercising, or working on his mental health, or sleeping extra long hours so his body and mind could recover. The best moments were when a friend dragged him out, not to talk about his problems or even do anything in particular, but simply to sit around and shoot the breeze, or watch a ballgame. It didn't even matter that he didn't like baseball that much. Sometimes you needed a lazy day to rest your mind.

He made a silent vow. He'd make sure she had some fun in the coming weeks. It was the least he could do to help her business – and Kari herself – thrive.

Chapter 5

After meeting the coffee roaster, Kari drove to her house. It would be easier to park the car there and walk to the café than to worry about finding a closer spot. Besides, if she was going to keep eating baked goods, she needed to walk as much as possible.

She was tempted to go into the house. Mom would be at work, Marley at the café, Brian at school. She'd have the place to herself. Lying down for a few minutes sounded like the biggest luxury in the world. She'd been working forever. She'd gone from top ten percent of her class in high school straight to college. There she took a heavy course load in order to graduate as quickly as possible and save money on tuition. She developed the café business plan as a senior project, and then she'd fallen in love with the idea and started to believe it might actually work. Since then she'd researched options, met with people, applied for loans, expanded her idea after volunteering at the animal shelter, done more research.

Since Brian's birth, they hadn't really taken vacations, other than to visit Kari's and Marley's grandparents or the annual summer camping trip before her father died. Kari couldn't remember the last time she'd been on a date. A year ago? Obviously it hadn't been memorable.

She looked longingly at the house and turned away. A few minutes of rest could turn into a three-hour nap. Sure, she was worn out, but she couldn't afford to take a break yet. Too many people were counting on her.

As she walked the familiar route to the café, she reviewed her to-do list. They were more or less on schedule. Employees had been hired and the background checks should be in soon. The health inspector hadn't managed to schedule their final inspection yet, unfortunately, but as long as they got approval before their open date, the delay didn't matter that much.

Kari let herself into the café. Domino waited right inside the second door, so she had to squeeze through quickly and shut the door gently to make sure she didn't catch his twirling tail. She crouched to pet him, and he lifted his head against her hand, eyes closed, purring loudly.

Rock music played in the kitchen. Kari stood, brushing her hands on her skirt, and crossed to where she could look through the metal grille blocking off the serving counter. Marley joined in the chorus of the song as she unloaded the industrial dishwasher. Kari took two more steps to see Colin seated at the table writing on a sheet of paper.

Kari smiled. The scene was so comfortable. They hadn't spotted her, so she'd sneak past and leave them to it.

Colin tapped the paper with his pen. "It's a big grocery list. Are you sure we should order all the supplies now? We already have enough baked goods in the freezer for probably a couple of weeks."

Kari hesitated. Should she answer, even though he'd clearly meant the question for Marley?

Marley dried her hands on a dish towel and leaned against the counter. "Why wait? Those are all staples, so we'll use them eventually."

"Sure, but the sooner we order, the sooner the bills come due. What's the monthly budget for food?"

"Kari gave me the account number for the restaurant supply place and told me to order what I need for the baked goods. She orders everything else." Marley hung up the towel and crossed to the table. "You think this is too much?"

Colin looked up at her. "She hasn't shown you a budget?"

"She hasn't said anything about money. She told me to quit my job waitressing last month and focus on getting the café ready. She hasn't given me anything to do besides put together the menus and bake, so that's what I'm doing."

Kari edged sideways. They'd passed the moment where she could easily join the conversation. If they looked up now and spotted her, it would be awkward for everyone.

"She said something the other day about how expensive this has been."

Marley huffed out a breath. "She hasn't said anything to me. She wouldn't. You'd think she was the big sister, the way she tries to take care of everything."

Now that she was out of sight, Kari could no longer see their expressions. She should keep moving, out of hearing, but somehow her feet had locked to the floor.

"I did get the impression she was trying to take care of you and Brian, and your mom, with this place. Not to mention all the cats."

"That's Kari, trying to fix life for everyone. She has to do it all herself. She'd never let *us* fix anything for *her*."

Kari gulped and crept toward her office. She'd learned why you shouldn't eavesdrop. You might not like what you hear.

Did Marley really think that Kari needed to be fixed? Did Colin agree? She didn't claim to be perfect, but Kari was trying to build a better life for all of them. Shouldn't that count for something?

She wanted to escape the building, but to get to the front door, Kari would have to go past the counter again. She considered dropping to the floor, crawling to the door, and pretending she'd just arrived.

That was ridiculous. More specifically, it would be ridiculously embarrassing if she got caught. Better to keep going to her office, close that door quietly, and hope that when they realized she was in the building, she wouldn't guess when she'd entered.

Her shoes squeaked on the floor. She froze.

Marley said, "Someone needs to teach that girl how to have fun."

Kari stepped out of her pumps, crouched to grab them, and crept forward.

Domino wound between her legs and meowed loudly, annoyed that she was ignoring him.

Had the voices from the kitchen stopped?

Kari rushed the last few feet to her office. She reached her closed door and turned the handle. The door opened with a *creak*. Had it always made that noise?

In the main room, a cat yowled, and another hissed back amidst the quick sounds of scuffling.

Kari leapt over the child gate. Her foot caught. She grabbed at the swinging door. Her shoes flew out of her hand and across the room, landed with a clatter, and skidded under her desk.

She'd forgotten she was wearing a skirt that restricted her movement.

She hung on the door, unhooked her foot, righted herself, and turned around. If they spotted her, she could pretend to be coming out to investigate the noise.

Silence.

"Cleopatra and Misty are bickering again." Marley sounded louder. She must have moved to the counter to see into the main room. "They're all right now."

Kari sagged with relief. Before she could close the door, Domino jumped right over the gate designed to keep out the cats. He rubbed against her shins.

Kari shook her head, softly closed her door, and crouched to pet the black-and-white cat. "I'm an idiot."

His meow seemed to signal agreement, but he rubbed against her and purred anyway.

She sat at her desk and opened her email. The background checks were in, so she scanned them. Most didn't have a lot of information, as nearly all the baristas were under 30 and didn't have much history. But they confirmed that people were who they said they were, had a legal right to work in the country, hadn't lied about their education or current student status, and didn't have criminal records.

The service also did a credit check. Kari didn't care whether somebody was eligible for a mortgage, but a decent credit rating showed a certain level of responsibility, at least in theory, and stable finances might make someone less likely to embezzle from the café or steal the other baristas' tips.

Background checks were a recommended business practice, so she got them. Was that so bad, to follow the guidelines? Did people – her own sister – see her as a boring automaton who didn't know how to have fun?

She knew how to have fun. She simply chose to do more important things first. She'd find plenty of time for fun when the café was up and running smoothly, in six months or so.

Or a year. Or two.

Maybe she really did have a problem.

Domino head-butted her leg. She pushed back her chair enough so he could jump into her lap. "You think I'm fun, right boy? Or are you part of this conspiracy to get me to have fun? You know, I'm not opposed to fun. I'm just—"

Trying to fix things for everyone. Not because her family needed fixing. They were perfect to her, every one. She still wanted them to have better lives. Didn't they want that too?

She shook away these thoughts and turned to the next background check – Colin's. His was more interesting than most, but it still only covered the basics of employment. These weren't "Investigate your boyfriend to see if he's a criminal" background checks; they were designed for businesses. They confirmed his age – 29 – and military service. They listed his former employer, but of course had nothing about his injuries, as potential employers didn't have a right to medical information. He hadn't worked in almost two years, but that made sense. He'd said he had been focused on healing and was now trying to slowly reenter the workforce.

The background check did list social media profiles, for those employers who wanted to see how their potential employees acted in public, but he didn't seem active there.

A good Internet search would probably reveal more.

She wouldn't do that, of course. Not only had she already gotten burned by spying on people, but labor law said that you had to treat every applicant equally, and doing an Internet search on him would be for her own curiosity, nothing more.

See, following the rules wasn't only for her own benefit.

She reviewed the rest of the background checks and didn't find anything that would cause her to reverse a hiring decision, so she sent messages to her new staff – *her new staff!* – confirming their start dates.

A text came in from Kari's mother: be there two minutes if you there.

Kari responded in the affirmative, nudged Domino off her lap, and went to her office door. Hand on the doorknob, she took a deep breath and practiced her smile.

Marley didn't look up from the kitchen table as Kari passed the counter. Colin was stretched out on one of the padded benches in the main room, eyes closed, with Cleopatra perched on his chest. Maybe perched was the wrong word – that cat must weigh seventeen pounds. Roosted? Squatted? Made herself at home?

Regardless, how could Marley not be all over a cute guy who let a big cat use his chest as a bed?

Kari met her mother in the tiny foyer between the outer and inner front doors.

"Hey, sweetie, I want to hear about your meeting this morning." Her mother peered through the glass into the main room. "Oh my. Is that him?"

"Domino? He's the black-and-white cat there. Definitely my favorite of this bunch."

Mom narrowed her eyes at Kari in a glare that had often caused her daughters to confess when they were younger.

Kari chuckled. "Oh, you mean the man. Yes, that's Colin. I gather Marley has told you all about him?"

"More than you've told me."

"She knows him better." And she'd get to know him even better, if Kari had her way. So what if Marley thought Kari was trying to fix her life. She hadn't heard Marley complain about being given this job, or the chance at a great guy.

A tap came at the door behind her, and Kari jumped. She turned and backed out of the way as Marley slipped in to join them, carrying a ceramic mug of milky coffee.

"Are you holding secret meetings without me?"

Mom feigned innocence. "I wanted to hear about Kari's meeting this morning."

"Oh, right," Marley said. "A coffee vendor or something?"

"A local roaster. Woman-owned business. It went fine." Kari wrinkled her nose. "You could practically hear the woman thinking, 'But you're just a baby!' I'd guess she was in her fifties."

"Well, you are a baby to someone my age, practically ancient." Mom pinched Kari's cheek.

Kari pulled away, snickering. She had yet to decide if she preferred meeting vendors in person to talking to them on the phone. On the one hand, you made closer connections in person, and it seemed to leave less room for misunderstandings. She got to study the items she needed to order, to judge quality. But on the phone, she could try to drop her voice a bit and maybe they'd think she was older. In person, people often thought her even younger than 24. She put on makeup for meetings, and even wore skirts and heels, but that didn't seem to help. She probably looked like a little girl playing dress-up.

In this case, the coffee roaster had reacted with the usual wide eyes when Kari introduced herself. The surprise was followed by indulgent amusement, which was better than some reactions.

"We talked about where they source their beans, how they roast them, and so forth," Kari said. "She started to take me seriously. I guess all my studying paid off." Her tastes ran more toward caramel macchiatos than straight espresso, so nuances were lost to her taste buds. But other café owners had warned her that some customers would care and ask questions, so the staff should be ready to answer them.

"Do they suit your standards for ethical behavior?" Marley asked.

Kari nodded. "They buy direct from small farmers, they support a tree-planting program, and they use recycled packaging." Not only did ethical business, social, and environmental practices align with her personal beliefs, it also seemed fitting for a café with a major goal of finding homes for shelter cats. A business couldn't exist without using energy and creating garbage, but they could do their best to outweigh the carbon footprint with good stuff. "I committed to using their beans for three months."

Mom's gaze returned to Colin. She craned her neck, but she probably couldn't get a good look at his face from that angle.

"Want to meet him?" Marley asked. She tapped on the glass.

Colin lifted his head. He slowly sat up, sliding Cleopatra into his lap. The two seemed to exchange words that weren't audible through the glass, and Cleopatra stalked off in a huff.

Colin crossed to the glassed-in foyer. Kari switched places with her mother. There really wasn't room for another person.

Mom opened the inner door a few inches. "Hi, I'm Diane. I'm staying in here to avoid the allergens. Just got my shots and don't need anything else in my system." She twisted one arm to show the red welt near her triceps where she'd gotten the injection.

"Nice to meet you." Colin offered his hand. "You have a couple of amazing daughters."

"I take all the credit." She shook his hand through the slightly open door. "I can't believe the girls haven't asked you over for dinner yet."

"Yeah, what's up with that?"

Kari hid a smile. Mom wasn't subtle, but if it helped bring Colin into the family, so much the better.

"Maybe we should have a barbecue to celebrate the last weekend before the café opens." Mom shot a stern look at Kari. "If my daughter doesn't have you all working the whole weekend."

"I think I can spare them," Kari said.

Marley turned. "What about you? Will we get your company as well?"

Was that a challenge to have fun? Kari glanced down, remembering the uncomfortable conversation she overheard.

A gray fluffball jumped over Colin's feet.

"Shadow!"

Mom turned to give her a baffled glance and Colin's brows drew together. Kari gestured at the gray kitten as he slipped through the slightly open door. Colin swore and reached down, but the door started to shut while Shadow's tail was still in it. Colin grabbed the door and hauled it open again.

Marley reached for the kitten with one hand as her coffee cup wobbled in the other.

Mom swung around, looked down at the kitten, and jumped back. She bumped Marley's elbow.

The coffee cup went flying.

Mom stumbled against Kari.

Kari fell back against the outer door and slid down as it swung away behind her. She landed in the opening. She sat up blinking and looking around wildly for the kitten.

Colin crouched in front of the partly-open inner doorway, fending off Cleopatra, who swatted at Colin's shoe lace.

Marley held Shadow against her chest. "Got him. Good thing, or Brian would never speak to me again. Sorry about the mug."

Kari wriggled to sit up so the outer door could close. She looked down at her coffee-splattered skirt and the broken pieces of ceramic.

Mom sneezed. "I guess that's my cue to leave."

Marley offered a hand up. Kari stood and shook out her skirt. She looked at Colin, her face as hot as the coffee had been.

"Tell you what," he said, "you wash up. Marley can make you each a fresh coffee, and you can taste our latest. I'll get the broom and dust pan and take care of this. I'll even do a hairball check." He turned away, chatting to Cleopatra as she prowled alongside him.

Yep. He was a good one.

Chapter 6

Colin got out of his truck and leaned against it. A short sidewalk led to a small house that looked much like the others on the street. Most had been converted to businesses, but clearly they had once been private homes, when this was a residential neighborhood. Signs offered coffee, bicycles, beads, CBD oil, candy, books, and formalwear rental.

Nothing about the neighborhood should send his heart racing. Nothing about the animal shelter in front of him should cause this burning in his gut.

He pushed off the truck and strode up the walkway. He paused with his hand inches from the door. Could he handle barking dogs and yowling cats? Would the sight of them in small cages make him sick?

He swallowed hard and opened the door.

A plump middle-aged woman with tan skin looked up from a desk with a dimpled smile. "Welcome. Can I help you?"

This front room held shelves with pet food, leashes, beds, and similar items for sale. The chairs in front of the desk could have come out of a doctor's waiting room. A door across the room had a glass window showing a hallway beyond. The animals must be back there somewhere.

He managed to smile at the woman. "I was hoping to see one of your cats. Samson. I'm not ready to adopt, but ... I wanted to see him."

She nodded. "I know Samson. We have forty-three cats here right now, and I can't remember all of their names, but he's that big, sweet boy who had to come back from the cat café."

"That's where I met him." Colin shrugged. "He made an impression."

Her dimples flashed. "I'll bet. Don't worry, he's not always like that. Sign in here, and I'll take you back. I'm Celeste, by the way."

He almost tore the paper with the force of the pen.

Get a grip. You're only visiting a cat. Make sure he's okay, and then you can get out of here.

She opened the door to the hallway and waved him through. The hall had a faint odor of animals, but more like what you'd expect from a house where two or three animals lived, not dozens. The left side of the hall had several closed doors. In between each hung artwork featuring animals. The right side of the hall had large windows.

The woman paused by the first room on the right. "We separate the cats by age. These are the older cats."

Beyond the glass, the room had cement block walls and a cement floor, all painted a light gray. But instead of cages, the cats perched on carpet-covered cat towers, fuzzy beds, or white shelves attached to the walls.

"The next room has the adults. Kittens are at the end." Celeste glanced back over her shoulder as she moved forward. "If we put the kittens up front, no one would ever get past them to see the other cats. But adult cats make great pets too."

She opened the next door. "Samson will be in here." She went ahead and blocked a white cat with brown and black patches before it could sneak past her out the door.

Colin entered and closed the door. For a moment he simply stood and breathed, commanding his heart to calm. No cages here. No animals in torment. Several cats lounged on their high perches. A brown cat stared at Colin with green eyes. It had its paws and tail tucked close, so it looked remarkably like a loaf of rye bread.

"What do you think of our place?" Celeste asked.

Colin broke eye contact with the brown cat. "It's nice."

Celeste flashed her dimples. "You don't have to sound so surprised."

"I was expecting more cages."

"If an animal has health issues, we may have to quarantine it in one of the closed rooms, unless we can find a foster who can handle the care. Once the cats have been health checked, most do better in the open area. Cages can be traumatic."

"Samson indicated something of the sort."

She chuckled. "The open area helps them socialize, so they'll fit into a family better, especially one that already has pets. Cats aren't always friendly with each other, but here each can claim its favorite territory in the cat condos. We get some squabbles, but that helps us figure out who should be in a one-cat home, and who will do well with other pets or children."

Celeste peeked into some of the compartments and hammocks in the three cat towers. "He must be outside. Samson likes the sun."

Colin followed Celeste through an open door into what was, in essence, a large cage with chain-link walls and a wire mesh ceiling. But sunshine shone through the nearby trees, dappling the space with light. Several large branches had been propped against the walls and wired in place. Colorful ropes hung from them, and other cat toys littered the ground.

"There's Samson." Celeste gestured toward a chest-high platform where the big Siamese lounged on his side.

Colin picked his way among the cats and toys on the floor. He stopped in front of the platform. "Hey, buddy."

Samson opened his blue eyes and his dark ears rotated toward Colin.

Colin tentatively reached out and stroked the back of one soft brown paw.

Samson slowly blinked but didn't move otherwise.

"I'll leave you two together." Celeste bustled back to the inside room.

Colin slowly moved his hand up to Samson's shoulder and gave a few strokes. "You're quiet today."

Samson yawned, showing tiny fangs and a pink tongue. Colin glided his hand gently over the big gray body. Samson watched him through half-closed eyes.

A minute later, Colin said, "Is that a purr I hear? Or do you have asthma? You sound like you're snoring." It was a funny sound, but not unpleasant. He moved his hand back to Samson's head, and the cat closed his eyes and pushed his head into Colin's hand.

"Good boy."

Finally Colin gave Samson a last scratch behind the ears. He didn't know how long he'd been standing there. He felt ... lighter somehow. More balanced. Totally relaxed, but alert and focused. Was this how meditation was supposed to feel?

"Thanks, buddy," he whispered. "I'm not ready to adopt a pet, I don't think. Maybe ..." He shook his head and turned away, feeling like he'd gotten much more out of the encounter than the cat, but at least he knew Samson wasn't permanently traumatized.

Celeste finished straightening a cat bed. "All done?" She escorted him out. "As you can see, Samson is normally pretty mellow and doesn't mind people or other cats. He does mind cat carriers though."

She sat behind her desk. "If you decide you're ready to adopt, come in and fill out the paperwork. Samson could be yours within twenty-four hours, if everything checks out. It would be nice for him to skip the cat café and go straight into a loving home."

"I'll think about it. How long does it usually take for a cat to be adopted?"

"Hard to say. Kittens go most quickly. Older cats take longer, especially if they have health problems. And black cats, because some people think they're unlucky." She shook her head at that. "A few people come in wanting something specific, like a tuxedo cat or a calico. Others choose the cat that seems friendliest when they visit. If we get a really cute picture and post it on social media, we might get several people wanting the same cat."

"So Samson could be here a few weeks, or a month."

"Or he could get adopted tomorrow. You simply don't know." She opened a drawer and pulled out some papers. "Why don't you take the adoption application with you. You can fill it out at home – if you decide you're ready." Her dimple winked at him.

He wasn't ready. But he took the papers.

Chapter 7

Kari let herself in the side door to the garage, stripped off her T-shirt and jeans, and tossed her fur-covered clothes into the washer. She rinsed her hands and arms in the utility sink before pulling on a clean T-shirt and track pants from the stack on the laundry table. Since the washer was now almost full, she started it running.

It would be nice if Mom wasn't so allergic, but Kari didn't resent the inconvenience. She was tidy by nature anyway, and with three women and a young boy living in a small house with one bathroom, keeping things clean and organized was the only way to find anything when you wanted it. Those habits would come in helpful at the café, which would require constant cleaning to minimize the cat hair and odors.

She went through to the kitchen. Marley sat at the kitchen table helping Brian with homework, while Mom stirred a pot on the stove. Pinto and sweet potato chili, by the look and smell of it. Kari was so lucky to come home to such cozy scenes. Still, she'd like her own place. Maybe, a few years down the line, a house. A husband and kids. But for now, an apartment would do.

If setting up Marley and Colin worked out beyond Kari's wildest expectations, would Marley and Brian move out? Kari couldn't leave her mother alone then. Her father's sudden death had hit them all hard. Mom had come through the worst of the grief, and they'd built a new normal around the hole he'd left. How would Mom handle living alone if both daughters and her grandson left in a short period?

That was future Kari's problem. Present Kari couldn't afford her own place until the café was a success. She'd secretly hoped that might be in six months, but she'd planned for a year and recognized it might take two. Now two seemed more likely. They'd already gone beyond her initial cost estimates and were bumping up against her worst-case scenario plan.

"Hey, sweetie," her mother said. "Dinner in half an hour. I was starting to wonder if you'd make it home in time."

Kari smiled, hoping her anxiety didn't show. "I wanted to go over some paperwork."

Marley looked up. "Was Colin keeping you company all this time?"

"No, of course not. After you left, we shared ..." She wouldn't mention the Rocky Road Fudge Bars, not in front of Brian. They hadn't left enough of the broken pieces to bring any home. "... cappuccinos."

Marley's eyebrows went up. "Oh, is that all you shared?"

Uh oh, was she jealous? Or did she merely suspect they'd gotten into the sweets? "He didn't stay long after you left. He's going to talk to a yoga teacher he knows about starting a class for yoga with cats. You two work together so well, maybe you should follow up on that with him."

Marley studied her for a minute. "I think I'll stick to the kitchen. Class scheduling is all on you."

Was Marley was annoyed at her?

Brian asked, "Are you going back tonight?"

Kari shifted her attention and nodded. "I have to do the evening feeding and check on everything. Once we're open, whoever is working the evening shift can take care of that, but for now it's all me."

Brian sat up straighter and fiddled with his pencil. "Can I go with you?"

"Sure, buddy. If you're done with homework and chores, we'll walk over at seven."

"You should call Adam to walk with you," Mom said.

"Mom." Kari managed not to roll her eyes, but she shook her head. "It's less than a mile through a safe neighborhood. We'll be home by dark. We don't need an escort."

Mom shrugged. "I was thinking we haven't seen Adam lately." She started pulling plates out of the cupboard.

True, Kari hadn't seen her best friend much in recent weeks. They'd known each other since childhood, cemented their friendship in junior high, and stayed close through college. Adam had become like a member of the family. Lots of people had assumed they'd be a couple at some point, but he was more like the brother Kari had never had.

Now that they'd graduated, Kari was busy trying to start her new business, while Adam had a great job doing something with computers that she didn't really understand. He'd promised to get the café's Wi-Fi working. She'd almost forgotten that. She had a line for her computer, but café patrons would expect Wi-Fi. Playing with cats wouldn't keep them from wanting to go online. If anything, the opposite, as they'd want to post photos, which was fine with her – free advertising.

"I'll text him," Kari said. "Not about tonight, but I'll see if he's free this weekend."

After dinner, she and Brian walked to the café. She'd chosen the location for its convenience to her home. Fortunately, both the college district and downtown were expanding, spilling over into what had once been a fairly boring street with medical offices, CPAs, and a nail salon. Several restaurants and cafés had moved in, along with a bakery and a store that sold fancy loose-leaf tea. Kari didn't worry about the competition, because the other cafés would lure people to the street where they'd see Furrever Friends Café, and she had something none of the other places did. Lots of furry somethings, in fact. Plus, only the bakery made its own baked goods, and it focused on breads and pastries.

Brian scampered beside her. "I can't wait to see Shadow."

"He is a cute kitten"

"Uh huh. He's my favorite. I like them all, but I like Shadow best."

"Kittens are especially adorable." She pulled him closer for a hug. "Little guys don't stay little forever though."

He squirmed away, but his crooked smile said she'd get away with such antics for a while longer.

The evening sun cast long shadows as they approached the café door. They stopped in front of the outer of the two entrance doors while Kari fished for her keys.

Something moved behind the door glass.

Kari gasped and jerked back, pulling Brian behind her.

Her heart pounded as she tried to make sense of what she'd seen. A burglar? That was hard to believe. Reflections in the glass? No, *something* had moved, and none of the employees had keys yet.

A dark brown shape, about a foot high, rubbed against the glass.

Kari blew out a breath and released Brian.

"What is it?" he asked.

"One of the cats got past the inner door." Kari frowned. "That door latches, but I've heard of cats who can open doors. I guess this is one of them."

Brian crouched and peered through the glass. "Cool. It's that big shaggy brown guy."

"Merlin, I think. He looks like a Maine Coon. We'll have to slip in without letting him out." She unlocked the door and opened it only far enough for Brian to squeeze through. Merlin backed up when the boy came in, and Kari slipped through and locked the door behind her.

She shook her head at Merlin. "I guess you are something of a magician. At least you couldn't get through the locked outer door."

He gave a trilling meow.

Kari bent to pet him, and he arched his back up into her hand. She straightened and led the way through the inner door. "You thought you were so clever, opening the door, didn't you? Did you get stuck between them?"

He trilled and bumped her calf.

They'd have to put a lock on the inner door. Until then, maybe she could find a wedge to put under it to keep Merlin and any other cats from getting through. The cats couldn't escape unless they figured out locks, but she didn't want them stuck between the doors all night.

She also didn't want the health inspector finding cats where they shouldn't be. The kitchen door couldn't be pushed open without unlatching the handle, but if Merlin could do that, they'd have to add a sliding lock, ideally one that opened from either side. Unbolting the door every time someone passed through wouldn't be convenient, but generally they'd have one person in the main room to clean up and supervise cats, while a barista stayed behind the counter.

The window above the counter had a grate that pulled down at night. During the day, they'd have to count on alert baristas and some of the tricks experts claimed would keep cats off counters.

She wasn't sure those tricks convinced the cats, but she hoped they'd convince the health inspector. Her plans had been approved in advance, but she hadn't been able to reach her contact in Food Regulations since then.

Kari sighed and headed for the cat bedroom while Brian searched for Shadow. The converted storage room at the back of the café held nine litter boxes – one for each cat, plus one, as recommended – against the walls. They'd have to double that when they increased the cat population.

Shelves starting two feet up held rows of cat beds, each with a food and water dish attached to the wall next to it. Every cat could have its own bed back there, if it wanted one. At the moment, Cleopatra and Misty were curled together in one bed. Apparently they were frenemies, alternately fighting and cuddling. Two other beds had single occupants.

The other cats had stayed in the main room. Ideally, they'd spend most of their time out there when people were in the café, but it was important to give the cats a private area. It wasn't fair to force the cats on display all the time, besides which, an angry or frustrated cat might scratch or bite.

Kari rinsed and refilled all the water dishes and topped off the food. Merlin and Cleopatra came in when they heard the food rattling in the dishes. Kari scooped the litter boxes. This could get old fast, but she wouldn't always be the one doing it. At least they had a sink back there for easy cleanup and handwashing.

She flipped off the light. In the main room, Brian was on his hands and knees peering under the long bench.

"Whatcha doing?"

He sat back on his heels. "I can't find Shadow."

Kari's stomach fluttered, but she kept her voice calm. "I'm sure he's around." Unless Merlin had let him through another door. Or they had a hole in the wall somewhere. Or he'd gotten into the ventilation system. Or, or, or.

But they'd been careful in designing the room. The walls were secure. The vents had slats close together and were screwed tightly to the wall. Furniture had been chosen to avoid holes where cats could get inside.

"Remember, we want to give the cats freedom to sleep, or play with each other, or visit people," she said. "It's not fair to bother them if they don't want to play with you."

"I know."

Domino rubbed against Brian's leg. Kari could hear the purr from across the room. That cat would be adopted in no time. Brian's brown hair fell over his forehead as he stroked the black-and-white back.

"I just want to make sure Shadow is all right."

"Sure." Kari started checking the higher perches that would have been out of Brian's view. "Here he is." Thank goodness.

Brian hurried over and pulled up a chair so he could peek in at Shadow. Kari quietly counted the cats to make sure all were still there. This would be even harder when they had 15 or 16 cats. She didn't have any door wedges yet, so she locked her office door and moved a table in front of the kitchen door to block the handle. Then she stood frowning at the front doors. She wasn't sure what to do about the inner front door, besides prop it open and be careful the next time they came in.

Brian spoke softly, but not so softly that Kari couldn't overhear. "I wish you were mine."

She came up beside him. "I know it's easy to get attached, but you have to remember, all these cats will be getting adopted, we hope. They'll go to homes where they'll be loved. But we'll get more cats in. You can enjoy all of them, but we can't keep them."

He stroked Shadow gently. "Grandma is getting those shots. Maybe we can get a cat soon."

"Someday, absolutely, but you've seen Grandma after those shots. She still gets red welts on her arms. It'll be a while before she doesn't have any allergic reaction. Maybe another year."

Brian heaved out a huge sigh. His breath ruffled Shadow's fur. The kitten gave an adorable, high-pitched meow and batted at Brian's fingers.

You're not helping here, Kari silently scolded.

"Shadow probably won't be here that long," Brian said.

"Probably not. And he won't be a kitten that long either." She put her hand on Brian's shoulder and he stepped down off the chair. Kari propped open the inner front door and they left the building.

Had she made a mistake? Instead of giving Brian a place to enjoy animals, had she simply ensured he'd have his heart broken over and over?

Maybe it would be good for him in the long run. Maybe he'd learn to guard his heart and wouldn't be hurt as easily in the future.

Or maybe he'd learn to guard his heart and would struggle to connect with anyone.

Mom and Marley had approved the cat café idea. They didn't seem to think it would permanently scar Brian.

Ugh. Being an adult was hard.

Brian looked back every few feet as they walked down the block. Maybe she should distract him — and herself — with a change of subject. One popped into her mind.

"You've met Colin, right? Our other baker? What did you think of him?"

"I guess he's okay. He looked mean that day they brought the cats in, but Mom said he was freaked out about the noise. She said he's really nice. He makes good blondies."

When had Colin made his famous blondies and why hadn't she gotten any? Kari pushed aside the thought to focus on the more important piece of information. "Does she talk about him much?"

"I don't know. Mom and Grandma talked about him the other day."

Interesting, and a good sign. Kari couldn't remember the last time Marley had discussed a guy. "What did they say?"

"I don't know. I was playing a game." Brian trailed his hands along a chain-link fence they passed. A large brown dog lying on the other side got up and barked once. Brian dropped his hand. "Good boy. It's okay."

They passed on to the next block. Kari didn't want to pry too much, but she really wanted to know what Marley had said about Colin. Brian seemed to be thinking, but whether he was thinking about his mother, Colin, Shadow, or the dog, was anyone's guess.

Brian shot her an oddly sly sideways look. "Do you like Colin?"

"Sure, he's great. He's a really nice guy." Maybe that was too gushing. She didn't want to make him suspicious by overselling his mother's potential boyfriend. Besides, she remembered Colin's panic attack with the screaming cat. He'd snapped at her when she touched him. In retrospect, she should have kept her distance, for his sake. Even under that stress, he hadn't reacted physically, so she didn't think he'd be a danger to Marley, Brian, or anyone else. Still, a nine-year-old boy could get rowdy.

"You know he was a soldier, right?"

Brian nodded.

"Sometimes people who've been in war don't like loud noises or crowds. It makes them feel unsafe. He might seem cranky or need to be alone sometimes. It doesn't mean he doesn't like us."

"Okay."

"I don't mean you have to be quiet all the time. Just ... maybe ... pay attention, and if he looks upset, leave him alone for a while."

"Like we do with the cats."

"Yes. Exactly." Kari had never thought of it that way, but maybe humans weren't so different from cats. "We have to get to know the cats, understand their personalities, judge by their behavior whether they want to play or be left alone." She bumped his shoulder. "I'll bet you do that with your mom sometimes too."

He peered at her from under his thick bangs. "I do it with all of you."

Kari laughed. "Smart boy. So you know what I mean. No one can be totally sweet and kind all the time. Sometimes we're tired or frustrated or upset. Colin might get that way, like everyone does. He's still a good guy."

"I know that." Brian skipped ahead. "He likes cats."

Chapter 8

Colin dropped out of his handstand. He went to his knees and folded forward into seal pose, arms stretched out along the mat above his head. He felt the stretch through his shoulders, back, and glutes. Sweat stuck his T-shirt to his back. He took long breaths to slow his heart rate.

He sat up and looked at Leslie, his eyebrows raised.

"Great job," she said. "Forty-eight seconds."

"Shoot. So close."

His yoga teacher laughed. "Do you remember when we started? Did you really believe then that you'd be getting close to holding a handstand for a minute?"

He grinned. "I was still struggling to walk, so no. I've thanked you, right?"

She glanced at the container of blondies. "Every week for the last six months."

"Those are experimental. Gluten-free. I think they came out okay."

"Maybe if I tell my kids that, they won't scarf them all. You know I have to eat one of those on the way home, or they disappear the second I get through the door."

"It's the least I can do. The physical therapists helped a lot, but their goal was to get me functional, not optimal. You believed in me." Colin rolled to his back and pulled one knee to his chest. Leslie moved into position and pressed on his shin to deepen the stretch.

After thirty seconds, he switched legs. For his right leg, she had to press against the back of his thigh. He was almost used to his right leg ending below the knee. He still didn't wear shorts often, and in public he mostly used the prosthetic leg that allowed him to wear a shoe, even though it wasn't as comfortable for fast walking as the one with the flexible carbon fiber blade.

It was ego, pure and simple. So sue him. He wasn't trying to hide who he really was, not exactly, but he wanted people to see him for himself, not make assumptions about amputees, or worse, "war heroes." Then he'd have to explain that he'd gotten through military service just fine but been injured while working in the private sector. He was grateful it had happened that way, because that company had better medical coverage, plus a payout for severe injuries. People didn't want to hear that. They wanted to say, "Thank you for your service," maybe pay for his coffee, and walk away.

He didn't think Kari had noticed his missing limb yet. He liked that Kari treated him as a regular, capable guy, and not someone who needed a job out of charity. Marley knew, but she wouldn't say anything, even to her sister. She understood how people could make assumptions based on one little fact, as if that defined your whole being.

Leslie moved out of the way so Colin could straighten his legs. He reached his arms over his head, feeling the stretch through his core. "I want to ask you something, but please don't only do it to do me a favor."

"If it's testing another new recipe, I'm in."

"It's not taste testing, though I'll bet we could sweeten the deal with some baked goods and fancy coffee."

"Make it a chai latte."

"Done." He sat up and told her about the cat café. "What do you think? Yoga with cats sounds a little crazy, but I know some places do it."

Leslie laughed, her eyes shining. "Cats, lattes, baked goods, and yoga? Dude, we will make a fortune. Or if not that, at least we will have a darn good time."

"Great. The café is supposed to open Monday. I think Kari will want to give it a few weeks for everybody to settle into their jobs before adding special events. I'll give her your number and e-mail so you two can start talking about a schedule."

"This woman who owns it, what's she like?"

"Young, only twenty-four, so obviously ambitious to be opening a business. A cat lover, of course. Really smart, and generous, but she works too hard."

"You like her."

Colin switched to a modified butterfly stretch and leaned forward over his feet, hiding his expression. "Well, yeah, and her sister Marley. They're both great."

Leslie was silent for a minute. Good, she was going to drop the subject.

Then she said in a singsong voice, "Colin and Kari, sitting in a tree. K-i-s-s-i-n-g!"

He raised his head to scowl at her. "It's not like that."

"Sorry." She didn't look sorry. "I spend too much time around adolescents. But sweetie, it's hardly the worst thing in the world if you are interested in this woman."

"I guess." He rolled onto his side so he could reach his prosthetic.

"You haven't dated anyone since I've known you, have you?"

"I haven't been ready." He busied himself attaching his leg.

"What are you waiting for?" She rose and crossed to the mini fridge in her yoga studio. She came back with two bottles of water and handed him one.

"Thanks." He took a drink. "I don't want a woman to have to deal with my issues. Especially someone like Kari. She has her act together, but this is a stressful time, and I don't want to add to it." He put the bottle down and double checked the prosthetic.

Leslie sat cross-legged in front of him. "Sweetie, being part of a couple is about dealing with each other's issues. You help her, she helps you."

"Sure, but there's a limit. When I first got back home, I'd freak out at the slightest sudden noise. I once threw a punch at my mother. *My mother*." The memory, fuzzy as it was, still made him queasy. She'd dodged, and he hadn't connected, thanks to his poor balance and slow reactions caused by the medication he was on. She'd forgiven him, of course, but he'd never forgive himself. No matter what he'd been through, he had no excuse to hit a woman, let alone his own mother.

Leslie took a long drink and recapped her bottle. "When's the last time you did something like that?"

"It's been a while." He'd freaked out over the cat Samson yowling, but he hadn't gotten physical. It had been almost a year since he'd really lost it, eleven months maybe. And nothing had been as bad as that time with his mom. "That doesn't mean it couldn't happen again." But how long was he going to wait? What magic number would suddenly make him confident he'd entered the safe zone? Did a full year somehow have more meaning than eleven months?

Leslie reached forward and put a hand on his right knee. Her thumb brushed the puckered skin at the edge of his prosthetic. He didn't flinch, as he used to. That had been one of the hardest things about working one-on-one with her, letting her see and even touch his injury. Now he could believe it didn't disgust her. He relished her touch, not in any sexual way, but because it connected him to another human.

Maybe he did need a girlfriend.

"You deserve to be happy," she said. "It sounds like this Kari does as well. If you two could make each other happy, what's stopping you?"

"Yeah, maybe. I don't know if she's interested though. Sometimes she's hard to read."

Leslie sat back with a sigh. "Well, matchmaking is not part of my job, so I won't pressure you." She suddenly grinned. "However, I am looking forward to meeting the woman who put that look in your eye."

She rose smoothly, held out a hand, and hauled him to his feet. They exchanged a sweaty hug before he left.

Colin drove home thinking about what Leslie had said. Maybe it was time to start dating again. Maybe he was ready.

But dating his boss? That added an extra level of complexity. It set up an imbalance in their relationship and might be why Kari seemed to get flustered and jump back every time they flirted.

What could he do about it? He didn't want to give up the job. He was having too much fun.

He didn't want to rush things and wind up ruining them. If he made a move on Kari and she rebuffed him, he'd gain nothing and working there would become awkward.

He didn't want to put off moving forward forever. He was in a good place, maybe better than ever before in his life, despite his problems. The counseling had forced him to deal with some issues that had existed long before his injury. Kari wasn't the only one who had a tendency to work too hard and define herself by her job. "Toxic seriousness" his therapist had called it.

Dating was scary, especially with someone he really liked. Maybe he should have started dating casually, through an online site, where he could back away with no harm done if things didn't work out on the first date or two. But he'd avoided that, because the rewards hadn't seemed worth the trouble. It didn't make sense to try that now, simply to get in a few "practice dates."

Every choice had risks.

Kari might be worth the risks.

You can't control everything. Relax, and see what happens.

Good advice. Could he follow it?

Maybe he was over-thinking things. The timing wasn't right to ask Kari to go out on a date, not with so much else going on. But he could do something nice for her. As a friend. As someone who cared about her well-being.

Once in a while he caught glimpses of her humor, and she softened around her sister, her nephew, and the cats. Most of the time she worked like a mule and kept herself tightly in control.

Humor was a form of therapy. A counselor had taught him that. Laughter decreased stress hormones and raised endorphin levels. It even boosted the immune system. It was literally healthy to have fun.

He'd struggled with that for a long time, but he'd learned to schedule time for relaxation and find things he enjoyed. Meanwhile, Kari had turned something typically relaxing – playing with cats – into a high-stress business.

He took the next right, heading away from his apartment, toward a place he'd passed but never entered. They had events where you could get a painting tutorial while drinking wine and listening to music. They advertised it for bachelorette parties and "girls nights out." They made it sound really fun. He'd sort of wanted to go to one of their open evenings, but he suspected he'd be the only dude there and didn't want that kind of attention.

Maybe they'd be interested in hosting painting parties at the café. He could schedule one for Kari and her family to try it out, as a surprise. She'd have to participate, to see what it was like.

A glass or two of wine, her sister and friends, a bunch of cats, and some low-pressure painting?

That was sure to get her relaxed and laughing. Sharing laughter brought people closer together.

How close could he get?

Thinking about it, he smiled all the way to the painting studio.

Chapter 9

Kari collapsed onto the bench that ran along one side of the big room and bent forward, hands covering her face. She wanted to cry, or maybe throw up. She'd made her plan so carefully. She'd followed it to the letter. Of course a few things had taken longer or cost more than the estimates. She'd built in buffer for that.

Not for this. They were supposed to open in a matter of days. New businesses couldn't assume they'd make a profit right away, so they needed every penny in the bank to survive the first few months.

Something butted against her shin. She uncovered one eye. "Hey, Domino. Sorry, sweetie. I'm not really in the mood."

The black-and-white cat rubbed against her leg and purred. She stroked her hand over his silky back and let out a shaky breath. "At least this part is true. You guys help relieve stress. But you can't fix this."

A door closed. Footsteps crossed the floor. Kari didn't glance up until two pairs of legs appeared in her vision. She opened her mouth but couldn't make words come out.

Marley dropped to the bench next to her. "I take it the health inspection didn't go well."

Kari leaned into her sister. She avoided looking at Colin as he squatted and rubbed Domino's head. He'd thought she had her act together. Not many people treated a 24-year-old woman like she might be capable. Even her mother and sister had wondered if she was diving in too deep, too quickly. Colin had never expressed doubt. Now he'd know the truth.

No point in delaying the bad news. "He says we haven't done a good enough job separating the animals from the food prep."

"Oh, honey." Marley hugged her.

"I talked to someone in the Food Regulations Department months ago! He reviewed the plans and approved them."

"How can they change their minds now?" Marley asked.

Kari sighed. "This guy says the employee who approved the plans isn't there anymore but obviously made a mistake or misread the plans. He says the pass-through window and glass door to the kitchen aren't good enough. A cat could still get in. This is a cat café! The people who come here aren't going to be upset if a cat gets near their food."

"What does he want you to do?" Colin asked.

Kari bit her lip, trying to keep her emotions under control. "He says we need a wall completely separating the food service area from the main room."

The inspector had suggested another very simple, very reasonable alternative. They could not prepare food on the premises. They could still serve hot and cold drinks, and sell baked goods that had been made and wrapped elsewhere. Many cafés partnered with a bakery to sell their goods. That way they didn't have to have a full kitchen, train all their workers in food safety, or pass as many inspections.

It would simplify things.

It would ruin everything.

"We're supposed to open next week," Marley said. "Could we even get that done in time?"

"I don't see how." Kari hesitated, and finally added, "I don't know how we'll pay for it either. Not if we want enough in the bank to keep paying expenses and salaries."

Marley wrapped her arms around Kari and held her tight. She said, "Maybe you should ask for another inspector. Someone else might approve this the way it is now."

Colin shook his head. "Too risky. Even if you got it passed this time, they'll send other health inspectors in the future. You don't want to get this guy again, or another one like him, and suddenly get shut down."

Kari groaned. "I don't know what to do."

Buying from a bakery would take away Marley's job, or force her to be simply a barista. Maybe they could schedule time in a community kitchen for baking, but that brought other challenges. Plus, she'd chosen this location, a former restaurant, because it had a full, large kitchen. She'd had to buy a new oven and refrigerator. If she hadn't spent money on a commercial oven, she might have money for the wall.

"Some cat cafés separate the café from the cat playroom, don't they?" Marley asked.

"Yes, but I wanted to integrate them. The whole idea is that you get to enjoy your coffee or tea while playing with cats."

"Does that have to change?" Colin asked. "Did he say people couldn't even take their food and beverages into the cat room?"

"No. I guess they don't care what people do after they buy the food and drink. Once it's their property, I suppose they could eat it off the sidewalk if they want. It's the preparation and sales that concerned him." She brushed at her eyes and tried to find a silver lining. "If we build the wall, maybe some people will come in for coffee and your amazing baked goods even if they don't want to play with cats."

But that didn't solve the problem of paying for the new wall.

Colin stood and paced away, studying the room. "I don't think you have to totally separate the two areas. You're going to build an interior wall in an already-sound building. The new wall doesn't have to be load-bearing. You could make it mostly glass."

Kari looked up at him. "I remember a picture of another cat café with a long counter where people could sit to drink their coffee and look through a window at the cats. They paid extra if they wanted to go in and play with the cats. I thought it missed the point."

Colin crossed the room, skillfully dodging Cleopatra as she tried to wind around his ankles. "You have plenty of space. You could put the wall ten or twelve feet from the café window and still have a big area for the cats."

The calico pounced at his trailing shoelace as he paced a line across the room. "Imagine a counter with stools along here, facing a window where people can look at the cats."

Kari sat up straighter and brushed hair out of her face. "I was trying to avoid that. Partly to save the remodeling costs, but partly because I figured the people who would go to a cat café would want to *play* with the cats. Would anyone really come in simply watch others play with cats?"

"Mom might," Marley said. "She could enjoy seeing the cats without getting exposed to so many allergens."

"Parents might like to sit out there while their kids play with the cats," Colin said.

Kari scrunched up her face. "That's not ideal. We want this to be friendly for all ages, but children don't always know how to treat cats properly. I was going to insist that the parents closely supervise their children."

"You could have a minimum age for kids going in alone," Marley said. "Maybe ten? And you could still insist that the parents are responsible for their children's behavior."

Kari stood and paced the room as Colin had. She tried to envision his suggestion. One half of the building would be the big playroom, with the back room for cat beds and litter boxes. On the other side of the wall, a wide hall would lead from the front doors past the counter where they served food and drinks, and then past her office to the bathroom at the end of the hall. The kitchen was behind the café counter, with an exit to a back alley.

It didn't sound bad. It could even be stylish, if they did it right. "If we have the wall across here, it would keep my office, the bathroom, and the front doors outside of the cat room. That would keep the cats contained. Even with the double front doors, I've been worried about someone letting a cat slip out." It would also solve the problem of needing the interior doors bolted against cats such as Merlin.

She put a hand to her stomach. She still felt queasy. "Any idea how much this would cost?" $10,000? $20,000? She dreaded the answer.

Could she meet with the loan company again? They'd been surprisingly helpful, despite her youth, and passionate about supporting small, local businesses. But she hadn't even opened the cafe yet. How bad would it look to go back and ask for more money, to admit she'd made a major mistake in her plans?

Add in the extra weeks it could take to get the loan, talk to contractors, finish the build.

Weeks of losing money.

"You need some quotes on a budget and timeframe." Colin looked around the room. "I wonder if we could do some of the work ourselves."

"We need a general contractor to make sure it's up to code," Kari said. "At least we're not doing new electric or plumbing."

Kari looked at Marley, who now had two cats on her lap and one wrapped around her shoulders. The sight made Kari smile. This was worth doing. She wouldn't regret it.

Maybe she'd have to max out her credit cards. That went against everything she learned in business school. She could be a business owner at 24, bankrupt at 25.

It was better than giving up now.

Colin pulled out his phone. "Let me make some calls. I have a buddy …" He turned away and tapped at the phone.

Kari hurried after him and touched his arm. "Ask if they take credit cards, or have a payment plan."

He nodded. His sympathetic smile made her suspect she was asking for the impossible.

Kari crouched and made kissing noises at the calico who had fallen in love with Colin's boots. She reached forward and tapped her fingers against the floor to get the cat's attention. Finally Cleopatra gave up trying to nuzzle Colin's work boots and batted at Kari's fingers. A couple of minutes later, the cat was trying to crawl into Kari's arms. Kari lifted Cleopatra and crossed back to the bench.

Marley smiled up at them. "One good thing, in times of stress we have quick access to cats and chocolate."

"Who could ask for more?" Kari tried to put on a brave smile. "Pia at the shelter did a great job choosing friendly cats. A couple have been skittish, but we certainly have some love bugs."

Marley brushed Domino's tail away from her mouth and looked down at the two cats in her lap. "I have no idea what you're talking about."

She patted the seat beside her, and Kari sat. Marley took her hand.

"It will be all right," Marley said. "We'll get through this together." She glanced across the room. "You got lucky when that man walked through this door."

"I guess." Kari stroked Cleopatra. "It's nice of him to help, but I wish I didn't need help. I thought I had everything under control."

Marley bumped her shoulder. "You don't have to do everything alone, you know. We're all in this together. I owe you for all the years you helped with Brian."

"You don't owe me for that!"

Marley sighed. "I didn't mean it like that. Look, forget about who owes what. Let's just say we're family, and we'll work it out together."

Kari glanced sideways at her sister, and then across the room at Colin. "Family, huh?"

"Colin feels like family," Marley said. "Sometimes I can't believe we've only known him a couple of weeks. He's like the brother we never had."

Kari winced. "Brother? Really?"

"Well ... he doesn't *have* to be a brother. Did you have another role in mind for him?"

Kari was hoping to get more of a brother-in-law.

Cleopatra rolled onto her back, exposing her fluffy belly. Kari resisted the urge to pet it, or worse, tickle it. She had several posters on the walls explaining the meaning of cat tail positions and other feline behavior. A cat showing its tummy was relaxed and possibly submissive, but not necessarily asking for tummy rubs. Instead, Kari reached toward Cleopatra's head. The cat rubbed her chin against Kari's fingers.

Kari glanced at her sister. "I'll admit, when I first met him and found out he likes to bake, I was hoping you two might ... have some fun together."

"We do have fun together." Marley opened her eyes wide. "Or did you mean *fun*."

Kari chuckled.

"I trust you no longer think he's only suitable for some kind of baking booty call," Marley said.

"Shh!" Kari glanced at Colin but he seemed focused on his phone call. "I guess he's suitable for ... anything."

It was hard to remember that Kari had originally thought Colin might merely be good for taking Marley on a few dates, breaking her out of her single mother rut and showing her a good time. He did almost seem like part of the family now. A very sexy part. Maybe she shouldn't be thinking that way about someone she wanted to set up with her sister, but she'd hardly set up Marley with someone completely lacking in sex appeal.

Once Colin and Marley got together, Kari would be able to put aside her own attraction. For all his flirting, Colin seemed like he'd be a one-woman man. He might still tease her, as he would a little sister, but all his romantic playfulness would be focused on Marley.

She blinked rapidly and rested her head against Marley's shoulder. Of course she was sad. Her business was falling apart. Her sadness had nothing to do with thinking of Colin falling in love.

He smiled as he crossed toward them. "All set. Greg will come by this evening to look at the place. I described the job, and he thinks we can get it done in a day, if we pitch in with physical labor and assuming you can be flexible on windows based on what's available right now. He'll give us this Saturday with him as supervisor."

"Wow, thanks." Kari bit her lip. She didn't want to ask the next question. "Any idea on the cost?"

"It's going to run a few thousand."

She nodded, swallowed, and cleared her throat.

"We can ask Mom," Marley said. "She still has money left from Dad's life insurance."

Kari shook her head. "That's Mom's retirement, and what she put aside for Brian's college. We won't touch that."

Colin pulled up a chair and sat in front of them, resting his elbows on his knees. He frowned at her for a minute. "I'm going to suggest something. Hear me out."

She looked into his golden-brown eyes and waited. Her heart seemed to pound louder than usual.

"I'd like to invest in the café."

"Oh, Colin, no! You don't have to do that. This is my problem."

He held up a hand to stop her rush of words. "Hang on a minute, I'm not offering this to do you a favor."

"Oh really? You've been waiting all your life to invest in a cat café?"

He grinned. "Not specifically a cat café, because I didn't know such things existed my whole life. But I already love this place, and I think your business plan is great."

She only rolled her eyes a little. "Yeah, we'll make a fortune. See how well it's going so far?"

He reached forward and tapped her knee. Cleopatra swatted at his hand.

"Don't sell yourself short," Colin said. "You've done everything right, but sometimes things still go wrong. I know this isn't going to be a billion-dollar business. It's not intended to be. It's meant to be a place where people enjoy good food and drinks and have a fantastic time playing with cats, and cats find their forever homes, and your family gets to be together."

He'd seen all of that. Most of it wasn't a secret, but she hadn't realized she was so obvious about wanting to help out Marley.

"I know it's a big decision," he said. "Take your time. See what quote Greg gives you. If you agree, we'll work out a contract. I won't try to change how you do things."

Kari glanced at her sister and back at Colin. "Would you still work here as a baker?"

"Absolutely." He smiled at Marley. "I'm having the time of my life." His gaze shifted back to Kari. "It will change things a little, me being a part-owner instead of merely an employee. It has to, but I'm sure we can work it out. If you want."

His smile warmed her. But change things a little? This would change everything. They'd be tied together in a new way. No matter what he promised, it was only fair to give him a say in how things ran if he invested. She'd have to give up some of her control.

Was that so bad? She didn't want a man to rescue her. She didn't want to need *anyone* to rescue her. But trying to build a business on her own was so hard. Marley and Mom were supportive emotionally, but maybe they'd been too supportive, trusting her decisions, not questioning her closely. They'd loved the idea of a cat café, the idea of a business where they could all work only a mile from home.

They hadn't been interested in the business details. Neither of them knew the full financial situation.

He wasn't asking for a half share in the business. She only had to take as much as she needed to install the new wall.

She was tired of being in charge of everything all the time. She wouldn't give over her control to him. But maybe it wouldn't be the worst thing in the world to have his support, financial and otherwise?

As if reading her mind, he said, "You don't have to do everything alone."

She met his eyes. "Okay. We'll work it out."

Kari put a hand to her chest and gave a heavy sigh. "I have some more bad news though."

Marley winced. Colin looked stern but gave a firm nod for her to continue.

Kari gave them a big-eyed, sad look. "You two are not getting this weekend off after all."

Chapter 10

Kari studied the contract in silence for several minutes. Finally she looked up and met Colin's gaze. Her eyes were an interesting color. Was that what they called hazel, kind of a greeny-brown?

"All right, I guess we have an agreement," she said. "In return for your investment, you have a fifteen percent ownership of the cafe. Any profits in the first two years will be returned to the cafe. I can buy you out for the original investment within that time, or with interest afterward. This seems fair. In my favor, really."

He wished he were closer. He wanted to study the color of those eyes. But this was business. "I promise, I won't try to take over, but I don't expect you to take my word for it. I think that lays out all the rights and responsibilities."

She fiddled with a pen. "It's not that I don't trust you. I was taught that it's even more important to have written contracts when you're working with family or friends. You don't want to ruin a relationship because of a misunderstanding or hurt feelings."

He wanted to reach out and put his hand over hers, but the desk kept her too far away. "Kind of like good fences make good neighbors."

"I suppose."

She looked sad. Sad at having to take on a partner? Sad at having *him* as a partner?

Or maybe simply worn out from all the work and stress. She signed the contract and pushed it over to him.

He signed and then stood with a smile. "Okay, enough business for now. Let's party."

Her brows drew together. "What?"

"Got a little surprise for you. They should be done setting up by now."

She tucked the contract into a file folder in a desk drawer. When she came around the desk, he followed her out of her office. They'd been in there half an hour, giving Marley time to help the painting instructor set up.

Kari came to a sudden halt in the big room. "What's all this?"

The instructor, a woman with long black hair, strode over to them. Colin said, "This is Symphony."

"What a lovely name." Kari held out her hand.

"Thank you." Symphony chuckled as they shook hands. "I suppose I should have been a musician, but I'm contrary. I run The Painting Place on Third Street. You may have seen it?"

"Oh, yes, you host classes and parties. I've never been to one though."

"Well, this time I came to you." Symphony waved at the easels set up around the room. Kari's mother, sister, nephew, and three of the new baristas chatted nearby. Marley gave a little wave.

Kari tipped her head to one side. "I don't quite understand. You know we're not open yet, right?"

"This is a demo, for you and your staff."

"I thought it would be fun," Colin added. He was paying for it too, but she didn't need to know that. "If it goes well, we can think about adding a monthly class here for customers. *You* can think about it."

She still frowned, little wrinkles crossing her forehead. "Is it safe? For the cats, I mean. Are the paints safe?"

"We have a number of non-toxic options," Symphony said, "but because some cats like to knock over cups of water or chew up paint brushes, we're using oil pastels today. I brought our sturdiest easels, ones we use in children's classes, so they won't tip over easily."

A couple of the cats were nosing at the easels, but most seemed more interested in the people. Brian sat cross-legged on the ground, bobbing a fishing pole with a feathered bundle on the end for Shadow. Several of the older cats joined the chase.

"Normally I use acrylic paints, because they have intense colors and dry quickly," Symphony said. "'Dries quickly' might not be ideal with cats around though. I'll research other options for the future. Maybe non-toxic watercolors, if we can find a way to keep the cats from nosing in the paints. Not that those paints would hurt them, but they could make a mess of the floor and you might wind up with cats that looked tie-dyed. For today, these are safe for the cats and people, and they clean up easily."

Kari's expression still seem tight and wary. Was she concerned about the safety of the cats? Or was she more concerned that he was trying to take over by pushing ideas on her?

Marley walked over with two glasses of white wine and handed one to Kari. "Relax. Trust us."

"You were in on this?"

"It was Colin's idea, but he asked me to help. We thought it would be a nice break to have some fun before all the work tomorrow." She lifted her own glass of wine. "Friends, wine, a little art, lots of cats. That's kind of the point of all this, right?"

Kari's expression cleared. "Right. Fun. I know how to have fun." She lifted her glass. "Let us eat, drink, and be merry, for tomorrow we shall work."

Symphony clapped her hands. "All right, let's get started. Everyone find an easel."

People shuffled into place. Colin found one on the end, next to Kari. Kari glanced at him, and then to Marley on her other side. "Do you want to switch?" she asked her sister.

Marley shook her head. "I'm good."

Colin winced. He wasn't doing well if Kari didn't even want to be near him. Oh well. She busied herself examining the setup, so he did as well. Each easel had a piece of heavy drawing paper taped onto the flat, angled surface. Clipped to the side was a cup holder with a half dozen colored oil pastels and some pencils.

Kari and Marley's mother, Diane, shuffled her easel sideways so she could see between her daughters.

"Mom, are you sure you should be here?" Kari asked.

"I took my allergy medicine and I'm not going to pet any of the cats as tempting as that is, and I'm standing right next to the air purifier." Diane smiled. "I didn't want to miss this. I'm giving myself two hours and we'll see how that goes. I think the shots are helping."

Merlin, the Maine Coon, sauntered up to Diane with his trilling meow.

She jerked her leg away from him. "Shoo, you gorgeous darling."

"It's no good," Marley said. "You know cats love people who don't want to get near them."

Brian darted over and picked up Merlin. He hauled the shaggy cat back to a shorter easel set up in the front row. He released Merlin, who flopped on his side. Brian squatted and rubbed the big cat all over.

Symphony clapped. "All right, who can guess what we're going to draw tonight?"

Brian's hand shot up. "Cats!"

"You got it. Now, I want to be clear. You can do absolutely anything you want. You don't have to follow my instructions. But I'll teach you to make something like this." Symphony held up a drawing of a black cat sitting on a tree branch against a dark blue sky with a rising moon. The shapes were simple and the overall effect was very pretty.

"I've given you the colors you'll need for this. If you want something else, I have other options. Please put your crayons back in the cups when you're not using them. We don't want the cats getting a hold of them and batting them all around the room. Now to start, you'll take the lighter blue crayon and make a circle for the moon."

Symphony sketched a circle on her easel at the front of the room. "If you're not comfortable drawing a circle freehand, I have some stencils. You can also use a pencil to sketch in the figures lightly first." She wandered among the students, making sure everyone got started.

Colin found the lightest blue of the oil pastel crayons, shrugged, and made a slightly wobbly circle off-center on his paper. He'd simply pretend the moon was not quite full yet. He wasn't too surprised that Kari waited for the stencil.

Next Symphony had them sketch in a light blue band an inch or so wide around the moon shape. Then they took a medium blue and made another band around the light blue, followed by yet another band in an even darker blue. Remaining corners got filled in with purple, or "dark violet," according to the crayon.

They used folded wads of tissue paper to smooth the colors and blend them at the edges. This resulted in a white moon circle against a blue evening sky.

Colin glanced around. Although everyone had done basically the same thing, the images already varied in how much of each blue they had, how big the moon was, and where the moon was positioned on the paper. Each person would wind up with their own unique result.

Symphony had them use a white oil pastel crayon to fill in the moon and sketch in light circles around it, adding highlights to the blue. "All right, now take your graphite pencil. It's time to draw in the tree branch. Again, you can choose your own shape. I recommend keeping it fairly simple so it doesn't get busy."

They watched while she drew a branch coming in from one side of the image. It split into a heavy branch slightly below the moon, and several smaller branches arching toward the top of the paper. "When you have an outline you like, fill it in with the dark pencil."

Kari leaned close to her paper and bit her lip, frowning in concentration as she started drawing her branch. She kept checking the teacher's version, until Symphony passed by and softly told her, "Don't try to copy mine. Simply do what feels right."

Kari took a deep breath and nodded. As Symphony moved off, Kari glanced at Colin and gave him a crooked smile. "You know this kind of thing isn't easy for a perfectionist," she said.

Great, he'd given her more stress instead of the stress relief he'd hoped for. He said, gently, "Practice makes perfect, but maybe in this case we need to practice letting go of perfect."

Her eyes widened. After a moment of thought, she nodded and turned back to her artwork with a smile.

Was she having fun? Colin couldn't say for sure. She seemed so serious even in her play. But at least she had a distraction from the business side of things.

It took a while for everyone to draw their branches. Marley finished quickly and went around topping off the wine. The branches varied from a few simple lines to rather complex. One goth-looking barista had a "tree" that looked more like a spider's web, in Colin's opinion. She'd also drawn a spooky face in the moon.

Meanwhile, Brian had chosen to make his moon yellow instead of white, and he'd added some green leaves to the tree branch.

"Now use the white pencil and make some highlights along the top of the branch," Symphony said. "That's the moon shining on it, and it will give a sense of depth."

Diane sneezed. As her body jerked, her pencil went flying. It hit the floor and skidded across the room, pursued by three cats. Laughing, Brian scrambled after it and returned it to her. Diane blew her nose. "Sorry."

Kari was half-doubled over, snorting. Colin met Diane's gaze and they shared a grin.

Kari was definitely capable of having fun. She simply needed a reminder that fun was there to be had.

Finally, Symphony had them sketch in one or two cats sitting on the branch. They used the black graphite pencil, so the black cats appeared in silhouette. Each cat had a teardrop-shaped body with a smaller round head. Little pointy ears and whiskers poked out to the sides. They finished by drawing a long, curling tail on each cat.

Kari leaned closer to Colin. "Pretty sure I've never seen cats with tails this long."

He whispered back, "Artistic license."

Finally, they used white correction pens to dot "stars" around the sky.

"I think my stars are too even," Kari said. "It doesn't look right."

"Add some more here and there," Diane said.

"Maybe a couple of constellations." Kari pursed her lips and got to work.

Finally, Symphony said, "Make sure your name is on yours. I'll take them back to my studio to apply the fixer, and bring them back here on Monday."

They peeled off the tape holding the images to the easels and spread each drawing out on the long table. The adults finished their wine as they admired everyone's images. Brian leaned his elbows on the table and yawned.

"We should hang these on the wall," Marley said.

Kari laughed. "Right, because they're such great works of art."

"They're nice, they're fun," Diane said. "They'll appeal to people who like cats, which presumably will be everyone who comes in here. If you decide to do more of these painting events for clients, this will show them what they can make."

Kari studied the art work. "You really think these will encourage people to spend money?"

"Absolutely," Diane said. "I haven't had this much fun in ages."

"But they're all similar. It's not like we did anything that original."

Symphony put her hand on Kari's shoulder. "You're missing the point. It isn't about creating work that could hang in a museum. It's about making something that you enjoy, that will bring back good memories. It's about having fun being creative and not worrying about whether you're good at it. I know, that's hard for a lot of people."

She held up Brian's piece. "When you ask children if they can sing or dance or draw, they'll all say yes. By the time we're teenagers, most of us say no. When we're adults, we'll say we have no talent, we only sing in the shower or in our car, we always wanted to write a book or paint or play the piano, but who has the time to learn?"

She put down Brian's art and gestured at the other pieces. "We think you can't do creative work unless you're super-talented and skilled. But it shouldn't be that way. Everyone benefits from relaxing and releasing their creativity sometime. It's about having fun."

Kari studied the artwork again. She turned to smile at Symphony. "You are absolutely right. We all need more fun. Colin, you're the hanging expert, so I'll let you find places for these on the walls."

She turned to the baristas. "Of course, you can take yours home if you'd prefer, but it would be nice to have some of these up for a few weeks."

They all agreed.

"We should set up a monthly painting-with-cats class," Kari said. "Maybe we can invite people who participate to have their art on display for the following month. Do you think that would work, Symphony? We'll have to work out a contract for splitting the income and so forth. You're supplying all the materials, so I assume you'd get the most."

"Yes, but I'll give you a reasonable deal." She looked around. "You're doing good work here. I may have to take one of these cats home with me. My kitty died six months ago. I haven't been ready for another, but I think now, maybe. I just have to decide which one."

Kari flashed a grin. "If you take two, they'll be company for each other."

Symphony laughed. "That would make it easier to choose."

"Brian is falling asleep," Marley said. "I'd better get him home."

Diane dabbed at her nose with a tissue. "I'll go too. My two hours ended twenty minutes ago."

"You can close up all right?" Marley addressed her question to the general area of both Kari and Colin.

"We got it," Colin said. He started collecting the empty wine glasses while Kari headed to the back room to freshen the cats' food and water. One of the baristas helped Symphony clean up while another went back with Kari.

By the time Colin made sure the kitchen was secure, the last barista was ready to carry supplies to Symphony's car. Colin shook Symphony's hand, thanked her, and bid her good night.

Kari took a last look around, her lips moving.

"Are you counting the cats?" Colin asked.

She shrugged and chuckled. "Making sure no one escaped." She yawned. "I guess that's it for the night."

They paused by the inner door and took a last look around.

"It looks good," Colin said. "You've built an amazing place."

She turned and looked up at him. "Thank you for tonight."

Their gazes caught and held. She swayed toward him slightly. Her lips parted.

He leaned closer.

Meow?

They looked down as Cleopatra flopped onto her back. The playful calico batted at Colin's shoelace and rubbed her head against the side of his boot.

Kari giggled. "I think she's in love with your work boots." Kari bent to stroke the cat. When she rose, she turned toward the door and slipped through it. The moment had passed.

Chapter 11

Kari walked to the café with her mother Saturday morning. Marley and Brian had already headed in. Marley planned to thaw some treats and get the coffee going for the volunteer workers. Brian said he'd start herding cats into the back room, although more likely he was playing with Shadow.

"It's going to be a long day," Kari said. "You have to give yourself permission to leave if your allergies are acting up too much."

"You let me worry about myself," Mom said. "I did okay last night, didn't I?"

Kari resisted the urge to mention the sneezing. Mom was certainly doing better than she had a year previously. Even more certainly, she was not yet ready for a cat in the home.

"I appreciate you doing what you can, but don't push it," Kari said. "I'm sure we'll have plenty of volunteers."

She hoped they'd have plenty of volunteers. Adam had promised to be there early. Colin would come for sure. After all, the place was partly his now, and he'd arranged for Gary the contractor to deliver the supplies and take charge. Colin had also invited a few other people, but would they show up for her, someone they'd never even met? Well, maybe they'd show up because Colin asked. He seemed like the kind of guy who was always helping people and making connections, as he'd done with her and the yoga teacher and painting instructor.

Kari hated to ask people for favors, and she didn't think many of her college friends would be adept at building an interior wall. Anyway, if they only had her and Marley, Colin and Gary, Mom as long as she could stand it, and Brian to fetch and carry, they'd manage. With too many people, they'd simply get in each other's way.

"You made the right decision, bringing Colin in as a co-owner," her mother said.

"I hope so. I think so." They'd shared such an intense moment the previous night. For a second, she'd thought he was going to kiss her. For a second, she wanted him to. That was not appropriate behavior between a boss and employee, although he wasn't really that anymore, was he? But it was also not smart behavior with someone she wanted to set up with her sister.

"He's a good man," Mom said, "and it's nice that we don't have all the risk ourselves."

"Yes." Many businesses, especially restaurants, failed in their first year. Kari did not want the café to be one of them. Too many people and animals were counting on her. It was helpful to have Colin's influx of cash, and he insisted it wasn't a burden on him. His background check and credit rating seemed to confirm that. Apparently, the private company he'd worked for in the Middle East paid extremely well, and he'd saved most of the money he'd earned, since they also provided housing overseas. That explained how he'd been able to go without working for the last couple of years. She'd thought maybe he was on disability.

She paused outside the café. Her insides were fluttering. Nerves about the construction? But they had a solid plan, a budget that worked, and expert help. That was under control.

No, she was nervous about seeing Colin again. She hadn't imagined that spark. In fact, looking back, she had to admit it had been there for a while.

Did she really want Colin and Marley to be together? She wanted the very best for Marley, of course.

But maybe she wanted Colin for herself.

She wouldn't think about it now. Whatever they might have or be able to build, it could wait. Getting the café ready to open came first.

"I feel good about this." Kari nodded. "We're on the right track. It's going to work out."

Mom draped an arm around Kari's shoulder. "Of course it is. For the café, and for you."

The door opened and Marley stuck her head out. "Are you going to stand out there forever? Come on, I can't wait to show you."

They paused in the foyer until the outside door closed and then went into the main room. Brian was dragging a feather teaser wand, luring a couple of cats toward the room with the beds and litter boxes.

Kari scanned the room again. She realized she was looking for Colin.

"Look." Marley grabbed Kari's arm and dragged her to the storage room where they kept the cat food and extra supplies. Marley gestured like a magician's assistant at about twenty bags of cat food piled against the wall.

Kari stared. "Where did these come from?"

"The pet store donated them." Marley pulled something out of her pocket. "And a check for five hundred dollars. All they ask is that we put a plaque on the wall saying that they're a sponsor. We can make up something fancy-looking on the computer and put it in a frame."

Kari slowly took the check. "It was on my list to reach out to pet stores. Somehow I never got to it."

"I know," Marley said. "That's why I arranged to see them. The manager was great. She's open to a long-term relationship with the café. They sometimes have adopt-a-thons, if we want to have a table at one. We can even sell coffee and baked goods." She frowned. "I suppose we'll have to check on the laws about that first."

Kari looked from the check to her sister. "You didn't have to do this. It's amazing, but it's my job to handle the finances. You're only supposed to worry about the baking."

Marley heaved a sigh and rolled her eyes as if they were arguing preteens again. "Stop it. We're in this together. For one thing, the success of this place is important to me because I love my new job and want to keep it for years. For the other, you're my sister." She slid an arm around Kari's waist and pulled Mom in with the other arm. "We're family. This is the family business. You know Brian will be begging to work here part time as soon as he's of legal age. Stop acting like everything is your responsibility."

Kari gave a weak chuckle. "All right, all right, I get the message. I'm allowed to ask for help once in a while."

Marley squeezed her. "We insist that you ask for help often. I know I haven't taken much interest in the business side of things. I'll admit, I find the baking much more fun. But you haven't especially made me feel included in the rest of it either. We've barely talked about the bakery budget, or what your goals are for profit, or how soon that has to happen. I love the baking, but I should know about the rest of it too. That's the only way I can make smart decisions. Because, you know, those rocky road fudge bars have much more expensive ingredients than, say, sugar cookies."

The food bill did add up, but at least it turned into profit, and it wasn't as much of a burden as the rent and all the food and litter for the cats. "I think we can afford the ingredients for whatever you want to bake."

Marley raised her eyebrows. "So if I wanted to make something with saffron and truffle oil, you'd be okay with that?"

Kari laughed. "I'd be fascinated to see what kind of baked good you came up with. And I suppose we could try selling something like that, if we could price it appropriately." She hugged her sister back. "Okay, I get it. I'll include you on all of the discussions and decisions having to do with the kitchen. If you're interested in the rest of it, I'm happy to share. I suppose it makes sense for all of us to know the details anyway. That way, if I get sick or something, anyone can step in."

"Of course it makes sense," their mother said. "We should start having regular meetings to go over everything. I'm sorry I don't have as much time as the two of you, but I want to know what's happening as well, and how else I can help."

"Handling the social media is probably the most important thing for now," Kari said. "I'm a little nervous about promoting too much too quickly, until we know that we can handle things, but we do need to bring in customers."

"I have accounts set up for the café on all the big sites," Mom said. "I found a program that lets me schedule posts in advance, so they'll come out several times a day, even when I'm at work. I'll need lots of photos and videos to post, and it might be best to give account access to you two and all of the baristas, so anyone can post when they get a good shot."

Kari glanced around the room. Colin should be part of this discussion as well. Did he want to know how things worked in the office, or was he really happy giving his money and staying in the kitchen baking? He'd insisted he wouldn't take over, but that didn't mean he wasn't interested.

It wouldn't be so bad to have other people involved in the big decisions, and the day-to-day details. Not because she couldn't handle it, but hadn't she been taught how important it was to have backup? What if she got hit by a car and was in the hospital for months? Someone would need to know how to run things. One of her business teachers had also warned against taking on so much that you got overwhelmed or burned-out. She hadn't reached that point – quite – but she had been letting some things drop, such as finding local sponsors. If she'd done that two months ago, or asked Marley to do it then, maybe she wouldn't have to take Colin's money.

No, she wouldn't second-guess that decision. He'd invested more than they were likely to get by adding up small checks from local pet shops or from an online fundraising campaign. Some cat cafés used those fundraising sites, but when Kari had viewed their pages, they'd only pulled in a couple of thousand dollars. Taking on a business partner with a substantial investment like Colin's $10,000 made more sense than working so hard for much less.

Where was Colin? She'd expected him to be there by now.

The front door opened. She needed to lock it. They had a sign with their official opening date on it, but that wouldn't necessarily keep people from wandering in off the street.

In this case, she knew the person. "Adam!"

Her best friend paused inside the second door, looked around, and whistled. He crossed the room with his loose-limbed gait and a huge grin. She stepped forward to meet him.

"This place is amazing!" He grabbed her and swung her around. Tall and lanky, he had almost a foot of height on her, so her feet didn't even brush the ground. He put her down, laughing. "I can't believe this is the first I've seen of it."

"You've been busy with your fancy new job. How's it going?"

"Good. The training is finally over, so things should settle down. I owe you some help on the Internet, as I recall."

"Yes, we need to make sure everything is optimal before opening to customers."

"Check. This place is going to be flooded, but we'll be ready." He greeted Marley and their mother, giving them each a kiss on the cheek.

"Adam, I have questions for you," Mom said. "Since you're the computer expert, I could use some advice on social media."

"That's not exactly the same thing, but I'll do what I can."

"You'll come over for dinner this week. We've hardly seen you in months."

Adam had spent so much time at their house growing up that he was like a brother to Kari. No surprise that Mom and Marley would have missed him lately.

As they got into conversation, Kari felt someone watching her. She glanced down. Sure enough, Cleopatra sat staring up at her. But somehow she didn't think that was what she'd been feeling. She turned.

Colin stood just inside the back door. Her heart gave a little leap.

What was he doing, simply standing there? He seemed to break out of whatever held him still and crossed to her.

Something about his gait caught her attention. Her gaze dropped to his feet.

His foot.

She'd never seen him in shorts before. She'd had no idea that his left leg was missing below the knee. In its place he wore a metal contraption with a flexible curve for the foot.

Kari swallowed and dragged her gaze back up to Colin's face. She smiled a greeting, but her face felt stiff, her eyes too wide. She couldn't think of anything to say.

He didn't smile back. "We're ready to start bringing in the materials."

Kari nodded. "Let's get the rest of the cats into the back room." Good. Something to do. She scooped up Cleopatra, glad for the chance to hide her face for a moment. What if he'd thought her shock was something worse, like disgust? Should she say something?

What could she possibly say? I notice you're missing a leg. No big deal, of course, unless you want it to be. Tell me how I'm supposed to act.

She straightened to see Marley watching her with a slight frown. Gauging her reaction.

Marley had known. She'd known about Colin's injury and hadn't said anything. Her narrowed eyes warned Kari, *Don't mess up*.

Kari's thoughts raced in circles, spirals, Mobius strips. Marley felt protective of Colin. Was she interested in him after all? Had Kari's reaction hurt Colin's feelings? She hadn't meant to. She was surprised, that was all. She didn't think any less of him – the opposite, really. He'd suffered a catastrophic injury like that and gone on to build a normal life for himself, so normal that she'd never even suspected *he was missing a leg*.

Act normal. She paused to introduce Colin and Adam. The two men shook hands and exchanged a few words of small talk, their posture slightly stiff and wary, like two dogs deciding whether the other was friend or foe. She did not understand men.

At least the awkward moment had passed between her and Colin. They could get on with their day and pretend nothing had changed.

Only, Kari wasn't certain yet if nothing had changed, or if everything had.

Chapter 12

Colin held the door to the back room, the one with all the litter boxes and food dishes. Kari kept her head down as she passed through with a cat. He shouldn't be surprised or disappointed in her reaction to seeing his injury for the first time. He hardly even knew how he wanted people to react. If they were cheerfully curious, it felt fake and awkward, as if they were saying, *Hey, I see you're disabled and I'm cool with it because I'm enlightened.* Serious and sympathetic was worse; he hated the pity. If they didn't show any reaction, he wondered what they were really thinking.

He should have given her some sort of hint ahead of time. It wasn't like he was testing her. Except maybe on some level he had been. If so, that was on him.

What was that line from *The Matrix*? Everyone falls the first time? It didn't matter if she was startled or even shocked at seeing his injury. What mattered was, did it make a difference in how she felt about him? Would she be afraid to get close to him?

She set that cat down in one of the empty beds and turned back to the door in time to grab an orange cat before it escaped. "Brian, any more out there?" she asked.

"I don't think so."

Colin went into the back room and closed the door behind himself.

"Okay, everyone hold still." Kari began counting cats.

Of course, even though they could each take a different bed, cats didn't work that way. Some of them curled up in pairs or trios. One sat on the floor licking its paw. The orange cat pushed at the door and meowed.

Kari finished her count and frowned. "We should have twelve, right? No, wait. We were supposed to get eight in the first delivery, but we had to send Samson back, so that was only seven. And then we got four more a few days ago. So that should be eleven."

She started counting again. She ducked to check the animal carriers that were sitting on the floor with the doors open, for cats who wanted more privacy. When she finished, she shook her head. "I'm only finding ten. Who's missing?"

"Do you need the list of names?"

Her nose wrinkled. "I should know them by now. Let's see, we have Merlin, Cleopatra, Misty ... Shadow. That's who's missing, the gray kitten."

She nudged the orange cat away from the door and stuck her head out. "Brian, do you have Shadow with you? Did you stick him in your sweatshirt or something?"

"Isn't he there? I put him back there, I promise."

"I don't see him. Take another look around."

Brian came closer. "I know he was back there."

"Maybe he snuck out again. Cats have a way of not staying where they were put."

Brian searched the room. Marley and her mother helped, and that tall kid, Adam, checked the higher perches. Finally Diane said, "I don't think he's out here."

"Shoot." Kari bit her lip. "Maybe we shouldn't have kittens here at all. They can get into spaces adult cats can't."

"You know he was here a little while ago, because Brian saw him," Colin said. "He can't have gone far."

Kari nodded. She scanned the room again. "I didn't miss him, did I? He's small, but not invisible."

Brian came up to the door and tapped on the glass. "He's not out here, Aunt Kari. He has to be in there."

Colin opened the door so Brian could slip through. The limited floor space didn't leave much room for three people. They shuffled places, and Kari bumped into Colin, her shoulder against his chest. "Sorry." Her cheeks seemed pinker than usual.

He lightly touched her back to steady her. "No worries."

She leaned into his hand. Was that intentional, or was she merely making room for Brian?

"Shadow," Brian said. "Come on, Shadow! Where are you?"

Mew.

"That's him." Brian scanned the room. "He's the only one who meows like that."

Colin started laughing. He pointed. "Look at Merlin."

The big Maine Coon was curled in one of the oval cat beds. It took a second, and then Kari and Brian laughed as well. A tiny kitten face looked up from Merlin's side. You could barely make out the little gray body amid all the bigger cat's shaggy brown and gray fur.

"All right," Kari said, "that's all of them. Now we need to get out of here without any of them escaping."

Brian leaned down to rub Merlin's head and give Shadow a kiss. "Good boys." Merlin gave his unusual chirrup, while Shadow patted Brian's cheek with a tiny paw.

They got out of the room without letting the orange cat escape. Kari locked the door.

"Okay, let's bring in the supplies," Colin said. "Marley and Diane, maybe you can start clearing the room. Put all the cat towers and chairs against that wall, and make sure there aren't any toys on the floor we could trip over. Brian, you man the door. Keep it open when anyone is carrying something through, and double check that no cats sneak out, just to be safe."

Kari gave him a grateful look. What did she think, he was going to assign a nine-year-old boy to carry heavy lumber and plexiglass panes? The kid needed a job to feel useful, but it didn't have to be physical labor.

The next task was to assign Kari an appropriate job. She was fit, but small. Between Colin and Gary, Adam, and two other friends Colin had recruited, they'd have enough men to do the lifting and carrying, and more people than that would cause a traffic jam. But Kari would be determined to do her share and then some.

He introduced her to Gary and said, "Kari will take the list of supplies." He turned to her. "Check off what we bring in. That we'll make sure we haven't missed anything, and you'll have checked the inventory."

She gave him a cool look as if she suspected he was trying to keep her out of the way, but she didn't argue.

They got everything unloaded and into the main room in under an hour. As the men brought in the supplies, Diane, Marley, and Kari helped organize things by type so everything was easy to find.

Finally Gary said, "All right, that's everything."

Brian let the door close. The guys stood for a minute mopping their faces.

"I'd say it's time for a coffee break," Marley said, "unless you'd like something cold? And maybe a little snack."

Marley headed for the kitchen. She opened the grate over the counter and served people through it. She had some hearty muffins packed with nuts and dried fruit, as well as espresso brownies and the cookie dough brownies. The guys ate like they'd never seen baked goods before.

"Thank you, ma'am," Jamar said. "That was the best thing I've had in ages."

"I'm advertising," Marley said. "I'm trying to convince you to come back soon and often, and to tell everyone you know about this place."

He smiled widely. "You can bet I will."

The work went quickly with Gary in charge. They set a chalk line on the floor to guide them in keeping the wall straight. They put down the base plate board, the side studs, and the top plate. They added a double header to go along the top of the windows. Several double studs with blocking supported the wall along the middle.

After a lunch of sandwiches, Diane and Adam retreated to the office to do on something on the computer. Colin wasn't sorry to lose Adam. The kid had worked with enthusiasm, but he clearly had never done any type of construction before. And for some reason, his easy affection with Kari grated on Colin's nerves.

Apparently, they'd been friends for years. If they felt romantic toward each other, they would have done something about it before now, right?

And yet, why wouldn't Kari want to date Adam? He was smart, with some kind of great job working with computers. Her family acted like he was one of them. He was good-looking in that lanky, puppy dog way, as far as Colin could judge such things. Adam had all his limbs and probably didn't suffer from PTSD.

There was absolutely no reason Colin should take an instant dislike to Adam. He was a nice kid, and Colin really had to stop thinking of him as a kid, because he was Kari's age. She simply seemed more mature, more ... everything.

Gary started framing one window, laying the pieces on the floor and quickly nailing them together. His nail gun made an almost steady tap-tap-tap, with an occasional deeper thud when he kicked a two-by-four into place. Jamar and Luis worked on another piece of wall.

"I'm amazed at how quickly this is going," Kari said. "I had no idea you could put up a wall in one day, especially with windows and a door."

"It helps to have the right tools." Colin gestured at Gary's professional nail gun. "Not to mention people who know what they're doing."

She stepped closer and looked up at him. "Are we actually going to finish this today?"

"We'll see about the painting." He gazed into her green-brown eyes. Such pretty eyes. "We'll be done tomorrow for sure. We spent more to get non-toxic paint that won't smell so strong."

Gary stood and gestured for Colin. Together they lifted the window framing into place.

When Colin turned back, he caught Kari looking at his artificial limb. She glanced up, gave him a crooked smile, and looked like she was going to say something. She didn't speak, but she didn't look away.

He stepped back to her. "It's okay if you have questions." He sounded hoarse, so he cleared his throat. "You can ask me anything, about anything."

She rubbed her lips together. He wanted to taste those lips.

"I'm not even sure what to ask." She looked down at his leg and back up at him. "Does it hurt?"

"Sometimes. Not as often, or as much, as it used to." He shrugged. "I can handle it."

Her lips curved. "Seems like you can handle anything." She glanced down again. "You haven't been wearing that the whole time, have you? I may not be the most observant person, but it doesn't look like you could wear a shoe with that, and I think I would have noticed it."

"No, I have another one that looks more natural. But this flex foot is more comfortable, especially when I'm really active."

"Why don't you wear it all the time?"

He stared at her for a minute. "Good question."

She held his gaze. "I hope you're not ... embarrassed?"

"Not exactly, but I don't want to be defined by my leg, or lack of leg. Sometimes it's easier to hide the damage."

"I guess I can see that."

She leaned a little closer and gave him a smile that warmed him to his toes. He even imagined he felt it in his missing foot.

She said, "You don't have to hide anything from me."

He cleared his throat again. "I'm glad." She wasn't freaked out. If anything, she was being nicer than ever. Was it because she felt sorry for him? Because he'd invested in the café and paid for this renovation? Because they were becoming friends? Or because she liked him the way he liked her?

She nodded once. "After all, we're partners now."

"Right. Partners." Partners in the business. But could they be anything else?

Chapter 13

Kari sat on the long padded bench, leaning against Adam, watching the other men put up drywall and install windows.

Okay, she watched Colin, if you wanted to be specific. He moved with confidence, even grace, despite the fact that half his leg was made of metal. What must he have endured to get to where he was now?

She felt terribly young and naïve in comparison. He'd seen much more of the world. He'd done and suffered things she couldn't imagine. He'd come through trauma to emerge the easy-going, balanced, amazing guy he was.

Why would a man like that ever be interested in someone like her?

Adam shifted beside her. Misty, curled in his lap, gave him a baleful look.

"Marley and your mom speak pretty highly of that guy." Adam spoke softly, as they were only fifteen feet away from Colin and Gary.

"Colin? Yeah, he's great." She didn't have words for how fantastic he was.

Adam grunted. "I guess, if you like that type."

Kari shot him an amused glance. "Are you saying he's not your type?"

"Ha ha. What I'm wondering is, is he Marley's type?"

Kari stiffened. "Why would you ask that?" She shouldn't be hurt that he'd assumed Colin would like Marley, and vice versa. Kari had assumed it herself. But could anyone even consider that Colin might like Kari instead? Was that so hard to imagine?

"I don't know. I thought ... She's been spending a lot of time with him, from what I hear. Is she dating now? I was wondering if she'd go for a guy like that."

Kari shrugged and tried not to pout. "She hasn't said anything to make me think she feels that way about Colin."

Marley hadn't said otherwise either. Would Marley tell Kari if she was interested in Colin? Or would she simply assume the field was clear for her and Colin, if she wanted him?

Kari should tell Adam about her feelings – but not here, not now, in the middle of everything.

Gary went to work with the nail gun. The noise put an end to any conversation below a shout, but it did not stop Kari from thinking about the issue.

Marley was closer to Colin's age. She'd had more experience with the world. Not that being a young single mother was the same as going to war, but they had both been through tough stuff. Plus they shared a love of baking. They probably had more in common than Colin and Kari ever would.

Maybe Kari's first instinct had been right. Marley deserved the best, and Kari was coming to realize that Colin truly was the best. Not merely for a "break the dating drought" fling, but long term. Maybe forever.

He deserved someone as amazing as Marley.

She tried to imagine the two of them together. Would it work? All she could see was her own misery, wanting what they had, wanting Colin.

She had to decide what she was going to do. Back off, stop thinking of him in any romantic sense, and help them get together? Or take a chance, let him know her interest, and see what happened?

Both paths seemed fraught with anxiety, danger, and potential heartbreak.

Now that he was a partial owner, she didn't have to worry about the imbalance of power that made it inappropriate to date an employee. But as business partners, they were tied together even more closely, which meant greater risk if something went wrong. Even worse, what if she told him she was interested, and he wasn't? Worst of all, what if he had to tell her he had fallen for Marley? That would be horrible for all of them.

The noise of the nail gun pounding into the big sheets of drywall stopped. The new wall wasn't painted, but it looked like a wall, with a door and lots of windows. The door had a large glass pane so people could see inside before they entered. Or rather, a plexiglass pane, Gary had said, so it wouldn't shatter so easily.

Jamar and Luis, who'd been on the other side of the wall, came through the new door. The four men huddled in conference. After a few minutes, Colin crossed to Kari and Adam. He was frowning. Was something wrong with the wall, with the building plan? She sat up straighter and scooted to the edge of the bench.

"We're done for today," Colin said. "We'll paint tomorrow. You don't need to be here for that. You should take a day off if you're going to open on Monday."

"I don't mind. Anyway, I'll need to come in to scoop litter boxes and feed the cats, and get them out of your way while you paint."

"I can take care of that."

"I don't feel right taking time off when other people are working."

One side of his mouth curved up as he shook his head. "You're going to have to get over that if you're running a business that's open seven days a week. You need to take care of yourself. This next week is going to be stressful for you, regardless of how many customers you get in." He leaned toward her and his gaze bored into hers. "Take the day off."

The rumble of his voice seemed to reach down to her belly, down to her toes.

Adam touched her shoulder. "He's right. You work too hard. You don't want to make yourself sick again."

Kari flinched and glanced back at Colin, hoping he hadn't noticed that *again*. All right, so once or twice –

maybe three times – she'd put in too many late nights studying and wound up getting sick. That didn't mean they should expect her to be so fragile all the time.

Still, they had a point. In any case, Colin was a co-owner. If he was willing to supervise on a Sunday, it would be almost insulting if she insisted on being there as well.

On the other hand, if she didn't come in, she'd miss seeing him.

Maybe that was for the best.

She gave him a bright smile. "All right, you win. I'll take tomorrow off, but I expect you to take Monday and Tuesday off. We have enough baked goods for the first month, judging by the packed freezer."

He held out his hand. "It's a deal. Should we let the cats explore the new setup?"

She nodded as she shook his hand, and he pulled her to her feet. They crossed to the back room, where Brian was sitting cross-legged on the floor with three cats crawling over him.

Kari tapped on the window. "Okay, kitties and kid, you can come out now." She turned to Colin. "If your crew can stick around, I'll order pizza, and I believe Marley found out what beer everyone likes and made a run for it earlier. It should be in the fridge."

"I think she's grabbing it now. Will your mom want to come back for pizza?"

"I'll call her, but she was clearing her throat a lot by the time she left. She's probably had enough cat dander for one day."

By the time Kari ordered the pizza and came out of the office, the now slightly-smaller big room was filled with cats. Some sniffed at the new wall. Cleopatra continued her love affair with Colin's boots. Gary dragged a feather teaser wand for two or three of the other cats. Jamar was taking photos or videos of the action, while Luis crouched and murmured to Domino, scratching the black-and-white cat's chin.

Kari paused to enjoy the scene. Even these burly working guys couldn't resist the allure of playful cats. If she wasn't careful, she'd wind up getting some adopted before she even opened. Not that finding good homes for cats would ever be a bad thing, but she needed to get more cats in to ensure they always had a selection.

She rejoined Adam. He was stroking Misty, who appeared to be asleep.

"How many cats do you have here?" he asked.

"Eleven right now. I hope to have fifteen to twenty most of the time."

He let out a low whistle. "That's a lot of cats."

Misty opened one eye to look at him, as if offended by his statement.

"From my research into other cat cafés, that's the right number," Kari said. "At any given time, some of the cats will be feeling antisocial and hiding in the back room, or simply napping. Imagine paying to visit a cat café and then not being able to play with a cat. You need enough cats that half a dozen will be ready to play or cuddle whenever people come in."

"I guess that makes sense."

Misty crawled across his lap to Kari. Kari scratched behind Misty's ears and listened to her purr.

"Plus, some people have favorite types," she added. "They think Siamese are the prettiest, or they once had an orange male who was sweet, so they like orange males. We want enough variety to help people find their ideal cat to adopt. Once in a while we might get a bonded pair and hope they'll be adopted together. The shelter helps us pick out a good variety of cats who are well-socialized with other cats and people."

"You've learned a lot since we worked on the business plan. I don't recall thinking so much about the cats."

"Yeah, we focused on the financial side of things. The last couple of months have been crazy, figuring out how to make the café and the cats work together."

"Sorry I wasn't there to help more."

"You helped in the beginning. I don't expect you to give up everything for my business." She leaned against him and yawned. "I have missed seeing you every day. We all have."

"Yeah? All of you?"

"Come on, you didn't notice how Mom pounced on you and demanded you come over for dinner? You don't think that's only so she can get computer help, do you?"

"No. Your mom doesn't hide her feelings."

"Are you saying I do?"

"What? No." He chuckled. "Well, you kind of do, but I think I've known you long enough to read you anyway. I just meant – never mind."

She gave him a stern look. "Adam, have you gotten weirder since you started this new job?"

He gave her his trademark goofy grin. "Nah. Only as weird as I've always been."

Brian bounced over to them. Adam offered a fist to bump. The male ritual greeting complete, Brian collapsed next to Adam and started talking at length about cats, especially Shadow, and how Brian couldn't wait to have his own menagerie.

Adam listened intently and asked all the right questions. Maybe he'd been worried about losing his status as honorary uncle. Adam didn't have any siblings, his father had been out of the picture for years, and his mom had worked two jobs. He'd been part of Kari's family since the two of them were in elementary school. Brian was the closest thing Adam would ever have to a nephew. Brian might have missed him in recent months, but clearly the boy hadn't forgotten Adam and didn't hold a grudge.

A rap on the door announced the arrival of the pizza. Kari paid out of petty cash. Thank goodness she didn't have to worry so much about a few dollars here and there anymore. Pizza and beer was a miniscule price to pay for the free labor they'd gotten, and Colin's investment covered all the supplies with plenty left over.

They pushed a couple of the small tables together and ate pizza off of paper plates. Several of the cats seemed to think the pizza smelled pretty good, so it was a matter of using one hand to eat and drink, and one to fend off cats.

Jamar and Luis both flirted with Marley. She glowed under their attention. Colin simply shook his head and said, "Forget it guys. She's too smart to fall for your lines."

Marley laughed.

Jamar slapped a hand over his heart. "You wound me, brother."

Marley stood up and struck a coy pose. "Boys, boys, there's no need to fight. There's plenty to go around."

Kari blinked in surprise. She'd never seen her sister play the coquette like that.

Adam sat up straighter and scowled.

Marley's eyes danced. She leaned forward and said in a low, seductive voice, "I promise, I have enough brownies for everyone."

Colin laughed.

Jamar rubbed his stomach. "Tasty as your offer is, I don't think I could eat another bite."

Marley patted his shoulder. "I'll wrap some up for you to take home. You all worked so hard today, and we're very grateful."

He jumped to his feet with a grin. "I'll help you in the kitchen."

"Grab the empties," Marley said. "We'll get them into the recycling before the cats decide they're toys."

Luis grabbed a couple of the empty beer bottles and scrambled after them. "Someone has to make sure you don't take more than your fair share of the brownies."

"I'll make sure they don't delete our dessert stocks too much." Colin followed the group headed to the kitchen.

Was he going after them to "protect" the woman he wanted? Kari thought Jamar and Luis were simply joking around, flirting for fun, but she wasn't the best when it came to reading men's intentions.

Merlin jumped on a vacated chair. Marley quickly closed the pizza box in front of him. She gathered the few remaining slices into one box and closed all the others.

Adam let out a long sigh. "I should get going."

"Okay." Kari shook herself out of her thoughts and turned to smile at him. "Thanks for coming."

Adam shrugged. "I didn't do much."

"You worked on the Internet and helped Mom. All I did was pass people tools and order pizza. I got the impression that if we all tried to help with the construction, we'd get in the way and do more harm than good."

He winked. "Keep that in mind when you're determined to work even when you're not needed."

She punched his shoulder. "Thanks for nothing. You're supposed to be on my side."

"Always." He stood up and stretched. "I have your best interests in mind."

"Yeah, everyone keeps telling me to relax and let them do things. I thought being a grown-up meant more hard work and responsibility. I'm getting mixed signals."

He looked down at her. "That's because you grew up a long time ago. You need to backslide a bit."

She stuck out her tongue.

He laughed. "Good start. I'll say goodbye to Brian and get going. Holler if you need me."

"Always." They'd been friends for so long. They told each other everything. Yet he didn't know of her confused feelings about Colin. Maybe she needed his outside perspective.

Later, when they had more time, when the two of them were alone together. After she'd had time to sort out her own feelings.

Maybe first she could get some hint of what Colin wanted, what Marley wanted. Because if they wanted each other, the best thing Kari could do was pretend she'd never had any feelings at all.

Chapter 14

Colin wasn't sure what to do with himself on his days off. He'd been having such fun at the café. Maybe Kari wasn't a workaholic. Maybe she'd simply found something she loved so much, she didn't want to do anything else.

He shouldn't have nagged her to take time off. But he had, so he couldn't break their deal and go in.

Colin removed the burner drip pans from the stove and set them in the sink to soak while he scrubbed the stove surface. Cleaning relieved stress. It didn't take all his attention, but it gave him something to do while his mind worked, keeping him in the moment, and he had the satisfaction of seeing results from his efforts, something that didn't happen when he sat cross-legged and said "Om."

The house felt empty. He needed a companion. He imagined Kari stretched out on the couch, chatting while he worked.

That might be hoping for too much

What about a pet? The experts sometimes recommended that wounded vets or others with PTSD or debilitating injuries get a dog. Dogs were needy. They forced you to get out of the house a couple of times a day to walk them, and they'd stick their pleading faces right into yours for attention, no matter how grumpy you were.

Cats tended to be more independent, but still, it would be nice to read or watch TV with Samson curled up beside him, purring, simply to know Colin wasn't alone in the apartment.

Colin had never realized how much personality cats had until working at the café. He thought of Cleopatra rubbing her face against his boots and chasing his shoelaces, and he chuckled. He pictured tiny Shadow curled up with Merlin, who was ten times his size.

Poor Brian, he'd be heartbroken when Shadow got adopted, but Diane wouldn't be able to tolerate a cat in her house for quite a while yet, with her allergies. So Brian was out of luck, unless this job paid enough that Marley could get her own place.

He'd have to talk to Kari about that. Clearly she wanted to help her sister and nephew, but Colin wasn't sure if Kari, or Marley, had an end goal in sight.

It was hard to believe he hadn't known any of them – not Kari, Marley, Brian or Diane, not Merlin, Shadow, Domino, Misty, or Cleopatra – a few weeks before. Now it seemed like his entire life revolved around the café, the cats, and that family.

Colin opened the oven door and examined the inside. He had a Teflon oven liner on the bottom to catch drips, so the oven itself was clean, but the liner was ready for a scrub. He pulled it out and added it to the sink. Twisting the flexible liner broke off most of the dried-on crud. This was definitely better than trying to kneel in front of the oven to clean it.

Kari had given him a strange look when she saw his prosthesis. Then she'd been extra nice, and he'd felt her watching him throughout the day, unless that was his imagination. She hadn't seemed disgusted or horrified, merely surprised and awkward, so maybe she could get over any squeamishness she might feel.

He set the oven liner in the dish rack to dry and looked around at his spotless kitchen. He could try some baking therapy to calm his racing thoughts, but he'd been doing so much of that at the café. If he was going to bake as a profession, he'd have to find another hobby.

So now what? Watch TV? Play video games on his computer?

He grimaced. Computers reminded him of Adam. Clearly he and Kari were close, the way she leaned against him like he was her favorite pillow. Marley had mentioned the guy before, but she talked about him as a nice kid she'd known all her life. Somehow Colin had imagined Adam younger, a slightly older version of Brian, even though he'd known Kari and Adam had grown up together.

Adam had some great job in computers, maybe even a security clearance. Colin had asked what he did, but within two minutes he was lost amid the acronyms and buzzwords. The guy was smart. If Kari wasn't interested in someone like Adam, why would she want someone like Colin?

Granted, Colin had a few things going for him. He had a nice nest egg in savings. He didn't think he was bad-looking. But the only reason he had a job was because of Kari's generosity in ignoring his lack of recent work history, training as a baker, or experience in the field. Otherwise, he would've been lucky to get hired on as a barista.

What kind of woman wanted a guy who worked at a café? Baking was a hobby, not a career for a serious-minded grownup. Kari might be young, but she was serious beyond her years, ambitious, focused, and hard-working. Colin hadn't given up on ambition, but he didn't want to spend his life chasing promotions and status.

He could see himself as a househusband someday – he hated the term, but the concept had appeal – taking care of the kids, cooking, keeping the house clean. Not having to face a high-pressure job, dealing with office bullies and sycophants, coming home wanting to drown the stress in liquor, chasing the next promotion, the next raise, having a heart attack by fifty.

He recognized the dangers of that lifestyle. Did Kari? Despite the supposedly-feminist modern world and all the talk of toxic masculinity, society hadn't changed that much. Most women, especially ones with their own ambition, wanted a guy with ambition as well. Colin didn't think he could do that for anyone. Not even her.

He sighed and got out his yoga mat. No point in pretending to be anything he wasn't. After an hour of stretching, he called his mother. Later, he called his sister and video-chatted with the kids. She had such a happy, chaotic household, with her husband, kids, and dogs. Could he have that? Spouse, kids, pets, noisy enjoyment?

Surely someday he could manage all those things.

Maybe he shouldn't wait for all of them. He could go get Samson.

If he wanted companionship, it was time to prove he could handle it.

This time, when Colin paused outside the animal shelter, it was simply to look around and wonder where the other animals were kept. During his previous visit, he'd hardly registered that he'd only seen cats. They must have dogs and maybe other small animals somewhere.

Right, the dog shelter was the building next door. It made sense to keep the species apart.

Would Samson get along with a dog? Colin wouldn't mind having a dog someday.

He'd think about that later. No need to plan his whole life in this moment. He simply had to take the first step.

He entered the building. A young woman, maybe only a teenager, sat behind the desk. She gave him a shy smile.

Colin cleared his throat. "I'm interested in adopting one of the cats. Samson."

"Please have a seat, Mister Samson."

"No, the cat's name is Samson. I'm Colin. The woman the other day, Celeste, gave me these to fill out." He held out the paperwork he'd completed.

The girl took the papers and frowned over them. "I can put your application in the inbox, but you'll have to wait for one of the regular staff to approve it."

He'd hoped to take Samson home that day. Having made the decision, the delay felt like a punch in the gut.

He could wait a little longer. What choice did he have?

She glanced up. "I just started. This is part of my required volunteer work for school credit."

"That's fine. Is it all right if I visit Samson while I'm here?"

"Of course. Do you know which room he's in?"

"The second one, adult cats."

She nodded and led the way. At the doorway, she hesitated. "I think I'm supposed to stay up front. Everyone's busy today. They had a big rescue, someone hoarding a whole bunch of cats. Some of them need medical treatment, and all of them need baths and flea shampoo."

"That's fine by me. I won't be too long."

She nodded and closed the door behind him barely in time to keep a black cat from slipping past her. Colin wasn't sure she'd even noticed.

His gaze immediately turned to the shelf where Samson had been hanging out before. The rye bread cat had claimed it and was grooming a back leg, somehow looking both ridiculous and imperious.

No surprise that Samson wasn't still in the same place.

Colin scanned the room but saw no sign of the Siamese.

He went outside. No Samson in that part of the enclosure either.

He must be in one of the cat houses or hammocks, tucked out of sight.

There, that glimpse of light gray fur –

No.

In the corner, a dark tail hung out of a round opening cut into a carpeted box. That gray shoulder inside the box seemed too dark, but maybe the shadows were misleading, maybe Colin hadn't remembered Samson's coloring accurately.

He peered into the box.

A strange cat looked back at him.

Colin checked every hiding place. No Samson anywhere.

In the hallway, Colin hesitated and then walked farther down. The third room was supposed to hold kittens, which Samson was certainly not. Colin didn't feel right going in without permission, but he looked through the window.

Lots of kittens. No large cats.

He moved back to the first room, the one for older cats. Had someone moved Samson in there? Maybe they'd made a mistake, or maybe they'd decided he was, in fact, older. Maybe he'd had a birthday.

Colin glanced up and down the hallway. He was alone. He slipped through the door and searched the room and the outdoor enclosure.

No sign of Samson.

The other doors off the hall were closed. They probably led to offices and treatment rooms. What else had Celeste said? Sometimes cats had to be quarantined. Maybe Samson had a health issue. Hopefully something minor.

Colin went to the front room. The girl looked up from a magazine and smiled. "Well, how's your kitty?"

"I couldn't find him."

"Oh." She stared at him.

"Do you have records of where the cats are? Is it possible he was moved to a treatment room or something?"

"Oh, right. We do have a book that tracks the cats coming in and out." She pulled a binder from a rack on the desk. "Let's see."

It seemed to take forever for her to flip through the pages. Colin was tempted to take it and search it himself.

She ran her finger down a page. "Samson, Samson."

"I know he was here three days ago, so perhaps start at the end and work back from there?"

"Sure, of course." She flipped forward and found the last entry. She scanned back a page. "Here we go." She frowned over the entry.

Colin clenched his fists so he wouldn't snatch the binder out of her hands.

"I'm sorry, you just missed him," she said. "He's out."

"What do you mean out?"

The girl shrugged. "I told you, I'm new. I don't understand all the codes. But he's not here. I guess someone adopted him."

Colin stared at her. His mind was blank.

She frowned and finally said, "Is there anything else?"

He shook his head, swung around, and rushed out of the building.

At his truck, he stopped and rested one hand above the doorframe. He dropped his forehead to the back of his hand. He'd waited too long. Samson was gone.

It was only a cat. They had dozens more cats in there at this very moment. Surely Colin would be able to find another cat just as good. How did you even define good in an animal? They were all good in different ways.

He heaved a sigh and climbed into the truck. Maybe later he'd think about a different cat.

But he'd wanted Samson.

Chapter 15

Kari went in early, even though it was Marley's shift, even though they had another barista scheduled, and even though they probably wouldn't get any customers first thing in the morning on their first day, when they hadn't started advertising yet. But she couldn't sleep, and she couldn't stay at home.

She could feed the cats, give them fresh water, scoop litter boxes, and make sure the big room was as clean as possible.

At seven, she let Marley turn the front door sign to Open.

They waited. She'd only scheduled one barista, a tall, lanky young man named Dustin. Marley had him make each of them a different fancy coffee drink, for practice. Then Marley and Dustin each leaned on the counter, chatting and sipping their drinks.

Kari went back to the big room and checked everything again. Merlin stretched out on the padded bench. Shadow batted at his ears. Other than the occasional ear twitch, Merlin didn't seem to notice.

Kari straightened the framed photos of cats on the wall. Cleopatra rubbed against Kari's leg. That affectionate cat would get adopted quickly. Domino lay curled in a hammock. Misty sprawled on the top level of a cat tree. A couple of the cats were still in the back room, but most had claimed spots in the café room. Feather wand teasers lay on several of the tables, ready for visitors. A bowl held toy mice.

Kari imagined Colin standing with her. He'd look her in the eye and tell her she'd done everything she could, and it was going to be all right. And she'd believe him.

How could she miss him when she'd seen him only the previous day?

She had to admit, she was falling in love with him.

She needed to talk to Marley.

She slipped out of the big room, gently closing the door before Cleopatra could join her. "Dustin, could you wipe down the tables and scoop any new deposits in the litter boxes?" It wasn't necessary, but it wouldn't hurt to get the staff used to using downtime for cleaning.

He saluted with his coffee cup and strolled away.

Marley sipped her caramel macchiato. "Should we have given you chamomile tea instead?"

"Ha. Probably. I need talk to you."

"So talk."

Kari straightened the plastic-wrapped rocky road fudge bars and espresso brownies.

Marley looked amused. "You know, it took Dustin ten minutes to get them in that fancy spiral pattern."

"Oh. Sorry."

Marley put a hand on Kari's wrist and said, "Don't panic. You knew this morning would be slow. Other than the sign on the door announcing our opening date, we haven't done any advertising or publicity. You made that decision for a reason. You wanted it to be slow this week."

"Right. I know. I'm not anxious about that."

Marley raised her eyebrows.

Kari blew out a breath. "Fine, I am."

"But that's not what you want to talk about?"

"Right."

"So ..." Marley drew out the word. "What do you want to talk about?"

Kari glanced away and then finally back to Marley's eyes. "Colin."

"Whew! It's about time."

Kari wrinkled her nose. "What does that mean?"

"You two have been dancing around each other since you met. Are you ready to talk about how you feel?"

Kari stared at her. "I was going to ask how *you* feel about him."

"He's great. I'm all in favor of it."

"Wait, what's *it*?" Kari shook her head. She had to be blunt or they'd keep going in circles. "Are you interested in him, romantically?"

"No, he's like the brother I never had. Like Adam is to you, I suppose. Even though we didn't grow up together, Colin and I had an immediate bond, but it's not romantic. Don't ask me why. One of those things."

"Oh. Good. I mean ..."

"I know what you mean."

Kari unwrapped an espresso brownie.

"Ahem." Marley tapped the plate. "These are for paying customers."

"Put it on my tab." Kari took a bite. "I skipped breakfast."

"Then this will really calm you down." Marley shrugged and took one for herself.

"When I met Colin, I thought he might be good for you," Kari said. "At first, I was thinking about a fun romance. As I got to know him ..."

"You fell for him yourself."

"No. Well, yes. But I meant I still thought you two should be together, only something more serious. I want you to be happy."

"I want to be happy," Marley said. "I am happy. More now than I have been in ages. I have a job I love. My son is getting more independent and turning into a cool human being. I have a loving sister and mother. I have a great new friend. What more could I ask for?"

Kari brushed brownie crumbs from her lips. "A partner?"

"Sure, that would be nice, but I've gotten along without one for this long. If the right guy shows up, and it works with Brian in my life, I won't turn him away. But I don't need a man."

"Of course you don't. No one does. Still."

"Still, they do round out a life nicely, if you get the right one." Marley took a bite of her brownie, chewed, and licked her lips.. "Does this mean you're going after Colin?"

Did it? She'd answered one question, would she be betraying Marley by pursuing Colin. But that didn't answer an equally important question – how did Colin feel about all of this?

Dustin opened the door to the big room and peered through. Kari scowled at him and he backed up.

Kari finished her brownie and wiped her hands on a napkin before she answered. "I can't tell how Colin feels about me. Sometimes he seems warm, and sometimes cool. But he's always at ease with you. How do you know he's not in love with you?"

Marley chuckled. "I think I'd know."

"Would you? I wouldn't. What about the way he was keeping those guys in check last night? He didn't want them taking their flirting too far."

"That doesn't mean anything. He didn't try to stop them from flirting with me, he simply made sure I was comfortable. You noticed those guys didn't flirt with you."

"Well, sure." Actually, she hadn't thought anything about it. Should she be offended that they hadn't shown the slightest interest in her?

Marley smiled and shook her head. "You idiot. You've got to stop putting yourself down and thinking everybody's better than you are."

Not everyone. Just Marley. "Okay, but they probably saw me hanging out with Adam and thought we were dating. Lots of people make that assumption."

"Do you think Colin thought that?"

Oh. Had he? How would he have felt about that?

Kari remembered Colin frowning as he came over to say they were done with the construction. He'd looked unhappy about something, but then she'd gotten distracted over their discussion of whether she should come in to work on Sunday, and she'd forgotten.

"I told him you two weren't a couple," Marley said.

"Did he ask?" That would be a good sign, right?

"No, I simply volunteered the information. I wanted him to know Adam wasn't a threat."

"A threat." Kari rubbed her face. She hadn't gotten enough sleep last night to sort through this. "I don't know what to do. How do I let him know I'm interested?"

Marley leaned on the counter. "The first thing you have to do is ask yourself, are you truly ready for a relationship?"

"Why wouldn't I be?"

The front door opened. An actual customer?

The man pushed through the second door and paused, looking around. Dustin came out of the big room to greet him.

Kari looked back at Marley.

Marley stretched closer and kept her voice low. "Because you're a workaholic and you've thrown everything into the café. If you're not going to have time for romance, for a partner, then don't start anything."

"Right. Okay."

Kari slipped past Dustin as he explained the setup to the customer. She paused at the door to the big room, listening. It was tempting to break in and take over, but she had to learn to let all of the workers do their share.

"Normally we charge five dollars to visit the cats, or that's free if you buy ten dollars worth of food and drink. For the opening week, we're offering unlimited cat time for five dollars worth of food and drink."

The man peered through the windows in the new wall between the café area and the cat room. He turned back toward the café counter. "I need to get to work, so today I'll stick with a latte. But I'll let my wife and daughter know about this place. I'm sure they'll be in soon."

"Check out our menu and let me know what kind of coffee you want," Dustin said. "You might want to look at the baked goods as well. That's Marley, our baker, and I guarantee everything she makes is fantastic." Dustin headed for the espresso maker while the man greeted Marley and studied the piles of baked goods.

Kari went into the big room. Dustin and Marley could take care of customers. The cats could take care of themselves, and Kari didn't want to wear them out playing in case other people came in and wanted cat time. The room was as spotless as it could be with eleven furry critters in it.

She had nothing to do but think.

She sat on the padded bench next to Merlin and placed her hand on his head. Shadow had curled up against Merlin's furry belly.

What did Kari want out of life? She'd had certain answers in mind for years. She wanted to build a business that kept her close to home, that benefited her entire family and the community.

That hadn't changed, but now she recognized that most of her actions had been focused on other people. What did *she* want, for herself?

Cleopatra hopped up on the bench and meowed. Kari moved her arms so the cat could climb into her lap. The calico settled down, purring.

Kari still wanted to run a business. She wanted to bring joy to the community and help shelter cats find homes. She wanted to help Marley and Brian, because she loved them. All those things made her feel good.

She also wanted Colin. His calming presence. His good sense. His kindness. His belief that she deserved happiness and should take time for play.

Could she bring herself to devote the time to a relationship? Could she give him what he deserved? Did he even want a relationship?

What did he want?

A man came to the door and paused, looking around tentatively. He held a cup with a teabag dangling out of it.

Kari managed to smile. "Good morning. Make yourself comfortable. Let me know if you have any questions."

"It is all right to have food in with the cats?"

"Cats can't taste sweet, so they don't care much for baked goods. They do like milk products though, so watch your lattes. And of course we ask that you keep an eye on your food and drink. Don't leave it unattended, and properly dispose of any leftovers."

He nodded and wandered through the room, pausing to look at the photos of the cats before he took a seat. Over the next twenty minutes, a few more customers came into the building, got coffee, looked through the windows, and left. Marley caught Kari's gaze, grinned, and waved. Some of those customers might come back later, when they had time to play with the cats. They might tell their friends. Imagine that, they were doing business, and Kari wasn't even devoting every moment to making it happen.

The man with the tea picked up one of the feather teaser wands. He dragged it in front of Domino. The black-and-white cat didn't move, but Shadow perked up, tumbled off the bench, and raced for the dancing feathers.

After a few minutes of play, the man looked up at Kari and smiled. He was probably in his thirties, with brown hair and a weary expression. His face was thin, almost gaunt, as if he'd lost too much weight. Yet when he smiled, Kari blinked at the transformation. He was handsome.

"You work here?" he asked.

"Yes. I'm the owner. Co-owner. My name is Kari."

"Zach."

"Welcome, Zach."

He turned in a circle, dragging the feathers as Shadow raced after them, until the little kitten pounced and rolled onto his back, biting and clawing at the toy.

"Thank you," Zach said without looking at Kari. "I needed this."

"All the cats are available for adoption."

His smile faded. He didn't speak for a minute. Finally he said, "I can't have a pet right now. That's why this is so special."

"Oh. I'm sorry to hear that." Kari's curiosity raced, but she didn't want to pry.

Cleopatra jumped off of Kari's lap and went to the man. She rubbed against his leg. He crouched to pet her. A minute later, he shifted to sit cross-legged on the floor and Cleopatra climbed into his lap. She put her paws on his chest and kneaded.

Zach leaned forward to rub his head against the cat's. "They know, don't they? When someone needs ..."

"Affection? Some of them certainly seem to."

He put a hand on either side of Cleopatra's face and stroked her gently. "You're a sweetie, aren't you? I wish I could take you home. But I can't."

He looked up at Kari. "I'm dealing with a serious illness right now. I can't be responsible for a pet until ... I know how things are going to go."

She bit her lip and nodded. "You're always welcome here. In fact, we have a monthly pass and an annual membership. You could come by every day if you wanted."

He ducked his head toward Cleopatra, so Kari barely heard his answer. "The monthly might work for me."

"We have a special offer this week. Half off this month if you promise to spread the word about Furrever Friends." That wasn't a bad idea. Good publicity. She'd talk to Colin about making it official.

In the meantime, she didn't know Zach's financial situation, but she could see he needed the cats. He couldn't be more than forty, and might be even younger than her original guess, if he was haggard from his illness, or the treatment. Cancer? She got the impression he wasn't sure he'd survive.

You never knew how long you had. It was easy to put off dreams and wishes for the future, focusing on working hard now to get everything in place. Kari had been doing that for years. Putting off dating, because it would take too much of her time. Avoiding new hobbies, because she had work to do. Planning her business, but not thinking about her larger life.

She'd never imagined starting a relationship the same week she opened her café. Later, maybe. In a year, or two. When things settled down.

Did things ever really settle down? She could spend the rest of her life planning for the future, and not living now.

Everyone had been telling her she worked too hard, she needed to have some fun. They were right.

She wanted to have fun with Colin. Maybe he wanted that too. It was worth a chance. She needed to let him know how she felt.

Kari knew what she would get from a relationship with Colin. He'd help her keep perspective, encourage her to have fun, make sure she had fun.

What did she have to offer him? Would he think, as Marley seemed to, that she'd ignore him in favor of obsessing over her business?

She wouldn't. If she knew one thing about herself, it was that she worked for what she wanted. She wanted Colin. She'd devote the time to making a relationship work.

But would he believe her? He needed more than a promise.

She needed to show him.

Chapter 16

Colin walked into the café Tuesday early afternoon and saw ... customers. One of the new baristas, a goth girl named Holly with dyed black hair and black lipstick, handed someone a large coffee drink. The place wasn't exactly bustling, but with even two people waiting in line, two more looking through the windows into the cat room, and several in with the cats, it seemed the word was out. They built it, and people came.

He'd have to ask Kari when she planned to start promoting the place. They should ask someone from the paper to do a story, if Kari didn't already have that arranged.

She probably did. He'd promised not to take over. He'd have to be careful about offering help, and not overwhelm her with advice she didn't want.

That was the downside of being this excited about something. He wanted to throw all his time and energy into it, but it wasn't his. He hadn't even been able to stay away through two whole days off. How could he convince Kari to find work-life balance, when he wanted nothing more than to be there himself, brainstorming ideas and working long hours making them happen.

Working long hours with her. He didn't know if she would ever be interested in him the way he was interested in her. But being close to her was better than being apart. If Kari saw him as more of a brother, the way Marley did, then he'd take what he could get and appreciate his new family.

He slipped through the kitchen door.

"Hey!" Marley gave him a sunny smile. "I thought you were off today."

"I am. I'm not here to work, unless you need me?"

"No, it's under control. We may eventually want an extra barista on the morning shift, but we're fine for now."

"Okay. Got all the baked goods you need?" Listen to him, practically begging her to ask him to stay and work.

"Enough for the week, I think, but if you want to do some baking later this week —"

"Yes, absolutely."

They grinned at each other, pure happiness at the success of the café, their part in it, and the idea of baking as work.

"What did you do on your day off?" Marley asked.

"Nothing much. Read a bit, watched some TV. Called my mom and sister." He wouldn't talk about visiting the shelter. Losing Samson still hurt too much.

"Cool."

They paused while the espresso maker ground loudly. Marley glanced at the plate of wrapped baked goods, which was looking scanty, and turned to the fridge. When it was quiet enough to talk again, she tossed over her shoulder, "What else do you like to do for fun?"

"I don't know. That's pretty much it. Maybe grab a beer with the guys."

"What about the movies, or going to a show?" She backed away from the freezer with a large pan and bumped the freezer door closed with her hip.

He shrugged. "I'm not crazy about crowds. Too much noise. I'd rather stay home and watch a movie on TV. Plus, then I can make my own popcorn."

"Sure."

She removed brownies and lemon bars from the tray, wrapping each individually. He resisted the urge to offer yet again to help.

"What about on a date?" she asked. "What would you do then?"

"I don't know." The last time he'd been dating, a colleague in the Middle East, they hadn't bothered with things like flowers and candlelight dinners. It had been years since he'd worried about impressing a woman on a date.

He might have to do that now. Would Kari want to get dressed up and go to fancy restaurants? Would she want to go to a concert or a play? She deserved to be pampered, but the idea of sitting in the dark surrounded by strangers made his heart race.

"Dinner someplace nice, I guess." He stuck his hands in his pockets. His shoulders felt tight. "Movie or a show if she wanted to, I suppose."

Marley stacked the new baked goods in a pyramid. "You'd do what you thought she wanted to do. What about what you want to do?"

What was she getting at? Had he misread the situation between them? They'd had an immediate connection, like they'd known each other for years. He'd been certain it was platonic for both of them. She felt like a second sister to him. But could she possibly be hinting that *she* wanted to go on a date?

She frowned and disassembled the lopsided pyramid. She glanced up. "One of the cats got your tongue?" She bobbed her eyebrows up and down at her joke. "You must have something you enjoy. I don't know, bowling or miniature golf or going to a baseball game."

"Again, crowds and noise. I worked security in the Middle East, and I got too used to looking for danger everywhere. A bowling alley would be too loud, too much like being under fire. Miniature golf might be okay." He tried to picture a miniature golf course. Fairly open, but maybe not too crowded? Little windmills and stuff?

He shrugged. "It's been years since I've done that. I'd rather watch a game on TV, and I usually do that with a male friend, or a small group. I don't think of it as a date thing."

He wanted to change the subject. He wanted to get out of there. But if Marley was hinting about wanting a date, maybe they should deal with it.

"Nothing loud and nothing fancy," she said. "I suppose as long as you don't date a woman who likes dance clubs or the opera, that works."

He chuckled. "I can't really imagine dating a woman whose priorities are dance clubs or the opera."

He didn't think Marley's were. He hadn't just suggested they'd be a good fit, had he?

"Why do you ask?" He tensed for her response.

"Merely making conversation." She kept her gaze on her new creation, a sort of lopsided spiral. "I was thinking if I wanted to do something special for a guy, what would it be?"

"You'd want to know what he likes, not what I like."

"Sure. Just trying to get a few ideas." She shook her head and disassembled the spiral. "I should leave the designs to Dustin. He's a real artist. We're going to have him do all of the writing on the specials board. Gorgeous handwriting."

"Right, I think he's an art major."

Holly the goth barista turned from the counter and gave him a long look. She swung back to greet the next customer.

Colin shifted uneasily. He didn't belong in the kitchen if he wasn't working. He was distracting them. He still wasn't sure what was going on with Marley, but this wasn't the place for a potentially difficult private conversation.

"Well, I'm going to play with cats for a while." Yet he didn't turn away. He wanted to ask if Kari was around, but he didn't want to be too obvious.

"Need a coffee?"

"Yeah, but nothing fancy. I'll get it." He grabbed one of the plastic mugs they used for in-house orders and filled it from the regular coffee pot.

He paused in the hallway to watch the customers watching the cats through the windows in the new wall. A woman murmured to her companion, "I want to come back this weekend when we have more time."

Colin grinned and went into the big room. Losing Samson hurt, but the idea of having a cat companion hadn't left him. He wasn't sure if Cleopatra truly had an interest in him, or if she simply adored the smell of his work boots. Regardless, she was a sweet cat.

Maybe he should get a cat from the shelter instead of depleting the café stocks, but he didn't think he could go back there.

He paused to look around. No Kari. Maybe she was in the office. Would she mind if he stopped by, or would she scold him for coming in on his day off?

Two cats he didn't recognize, mostly white with some beige and black patches, lay face to face batting at each other's heads. One of them put his jaws around the other's face, but it seemed to be light play-fighting. The two looked so much alike they were probably siblings.

A thin, rather haggard looking guy sat at a table with a cup of tea and a laptop. Domino sprawled half on the table and half on the laptop. The guy couldn't possibly be getting much work done that way, but maybe he didn't mind.

A woman tapped on her phone while two girls, maybe eight and ten, dragged a feather toy for Shadow and whatever other cats decided to join in.

Cleopatra sat on the bench, licking one paw and rubbing it over her head. She spotted Colin and hopped down, trotting up to him with a friendly mew. He crouched to pet her. She pushed her head up into his hand. Maybe it wasn't only his boots that had appeal.

The door to the room with the litter boxes opened. Colin's heart gave a hopeful leap even before Kari stepped out. He couldn't contain his smile as she approached.

She grinned back.

Cleopatra bumped his knee, and Colin sat back on the floor. That was more comfortable with his prosthesis anyway, and sitting made it easier to look up at Kari.

"Well?" he said. "It seems like the café is a success."

"I know, right? I can't believe people are already finding us." She leaned closer and jerked her head toward the gaunt man. "His second visit already," she whispered. "Our first monthly membership customer. He wants to spend time with cats, but he can't adopt right now. I'm worried about those little girls though. We might lose Shadow already."

Colin grimaced. "Brian will be devastated. But you'll bring in more cats, and he'll adore them all. The shelter will be glad to resupply you, right?"

"Of course. We want to find the cats permanent homes." She glanced down to where Cleopatra had flopped on the floor and was rubbing her face against Colin's boot. "But we'll miss these as they go."

"About that ..." He put his hand on Cleopatra's shoulder. "I was thinking of stealing this one."

"I think you and your boots would make her very happy."

Marley's questions had him wondering what Kari did for fun. He leaned back on his hands to more easily look up at her. "How was your Sunday?"

She opened her mouth.

Bzzzz.

She pulled her phone out of her pocket and studied it a minute. She leaned to where she could see through the window to the café counter and made some complicated response with her hand and face, presumably aimed at Marley.

"Sorry." Kari pulled a chair over and sat, elbows on her knees, so her face was closer to his level. Good, she didn't have to run off and deal with something.

"Where were we? Oh, right, Sunday. It was quiet." She shrugged. "I just ... thought about things. And I hope you noticed, I did not come in to check on you."

"Kari. I didn't mean to kick you out of your own place, or make you feel unwanted. I was trying –"

She smiled and shook her head. "No apologies necessary. I know what you were trying to do, and you were right. I will burn myself out, so I give you permission to nag me to stop."

"Not nag." He gave her what he hoped was a charming smile. "Persuade. Encourage."

"Uh huh. Whatever helps you sleep at night."

"Seriously, I don't want you to think I didn't want you around. You love your work, and I get that. I'd love to spend all my time here too."

"About that ..." She looked away.

Oh no. She was going to tell him she didn't want him there so much. His small investment didn't give him the right to act like this was his place. He was supposed to be a silent owner, and he'd been too loud. He should stay in the kitchen with Marley, or stay away entirely.

He shifted his weight and rested one hand on Cleopatra's side, as if her presence could bring him strength.

Kari looked back at him. "Since we're doing so well, I've decided to move up our official grand opening to Saturday. We'll close early Friday evening, at seven, to do some prep. Do you mind staying late that evening?"

He felt like he'd been given a reprieve from a sentence of solitary confinement. "Of course. That is, of course I'll stay late. I don't mind at all." He grinned so hard, he probably looked like an idiot.

"Fantastic. Wear comfortable clothes."

"I always do. Not that I couldn't dress up, if the occasion calls for it." If she wanted him to, he'd give it a try.

But one of the reasons he liked Kari was that she looked and acted casual. Seeing her now, he realized his earlier worries had been foolish. He couldn't imagine her demanding that he get dressed up and expose himself to crowds and noise. See how she reacted over his breakdown with Samson's cries. She'd offered Colin space and sympathy. She hadn't demanded that he "pull himself together" or "face his fears."

He could probably even tell her how he felt about missing out on adopting Samson, and she'd understand.

A pale shape moved in the corner of his vision. A light gray cat with a dark face and paws trotted over, tail held high.

It couldn't be.

It was.

Samson.

The cat came up, stared right into Colin's face, meowed, and put a paw on Colin's knee.

Colin leaned back, and Samson crawled into his lap. The Siamese playfully swiped a paw at Cleopatra.

Colin reached for Samson, almost afraid to find nothing there despite the noticeable weight in his lap. His hand settled on a soft, warm mound.

"It's him." Colin cleared his throat. "Samson."

"We got him yesterday," Kari said. "You'll see a few new faces. We had to use special delivery for this guy. Since he hated the cat carrier so much, we put him in a harness for safety and then in a cardboard box. Like most cats, he finds a cardboard box the height of luxury. I held him in my lap while Mom drove me over."

Kari crouched in front of them and scratched behind Samson's ears. The cat closed his eyes and purred. "I couldn't stop thinking about him." Her gaze rose to meet Colin's. "No cat left behind."

"I couldn't stop thinking about him either." His voice came out husky. He felt like some missing piece of him had slotted back into place.

Cleopatra sprawled on her side and tugged at Colin's shoelace, which was quickly becoming untied. Samson batted at her paws.

"I think he already has a girlfriend," Kari said. "Or maybe it's a love triangle, since she's more obsessed with your boots."

Colin swallowed hard. "Can I have him? Both of them? I know you just got him here, and you went to some trouble to do that, but ... I filled out the paperwork at the shelter, but he was gone."

She lightly touched his knee. "Of course. I didn't know you felt that way about Samson, or I would've told you the plan."

He chuckled lightly. "You mean when I fled the room when I met him, you couldn't tell he was really my soul mate?"

An odd expression flitted across her face. "We don't always know at first, do we?" She stood and brushed her hands on her jeans. "Well, if you want him, or both of them, I'll let the shelter know. Good thing I got more cats yesterday or we might run out by the end of the week."

"You're sure it's all right?" Probably a funny question to ask when he had an arm curled protectively around each cat.

"Colin." She smiled down at him. "Whatever you want is all right. Whatever you need, I want you to have."

She ducked her head and turned away before he could answer.

Chapter 17

Friday evening at 6:30, Kari rushed through chores. She scooped litter boxes, somehow flinging used litter across the floor. No matter. The floor had to be swept anyway, and in the morning, before they opened, each litter box would be emptied and refilled, and the floor mopped.

She scrubbed her hands at the sink back there before topping off the cats' food dishes. Whoops, she managed to dump half the food outside that bowl. She scooped most of it back in, turned away, and knocked over another food bowl she hadn't latched into its holder.

She blew out a long breath. She had to calm down, slow down.

Refilling the water dishes, she splashed water across the floor.

Kari sighed. Oh well, she'd mop the floor now and get the rest of that spilled kitty litter.

Perhaps she was a tiny bit nervous.

Her body buzzed with it. She wanted to flee the café and run about five miles, or until she collapsed gasping on the ground, which wouldn't take five miles.

She finished the chores at 6:50. Kari paused by a cat hammock overflowing with pale gray fur. They'd agreed that Colin would take Samson and Cleopatra home on Sunday, so the café would have plenty of friendly cats for the opening. But they'd added a label of "Adopted" to their photos on the wall.

Kari stroked Samson and tried to breathe. He started purring and she stopped feeling lightheaded.

The grand opening would start in about 12 hours, but that didn't worry her, that was under control. The baristas would keep the espresso maker running and the cat room clean as people came and went. Marley and Colin had baked up a storm for two days. Marley had the great idea of offering a tasting plate with small pieces of five baked goods for five dollars. Customers could then vote on their favorites. Kari's mouth watered simply remembering the pans of delicacies ready for the morning.

The social media campaign was running and Mom had invited reporters. A woman from the paper had promised to stop by. The local TV station might even come. All good news.

6:55. Kari addressed the few remaining customers. "We're closing in five minutes. Thanks so much for coming." She stopped herself from adding, *Now get out!*

A little boy said, "Awww," and whined to the woman accompanying him. His sister didn't put down the feather teaser wand that had Domino dancing.

Kari crouched in front of the family. "I hope you'll come back again. If you visit tomorrow, we'll have special games and give out prizes."

The boy sat up straighter. "A kitty?"

Kari chuckled as the woman moaned and shook her head.

"No, sorry," Kari said. "You'd need permission to take home a cat, and you'd have to apply to the shelter. But we'll give out some things with pictures of cats on them."

They planned to set up a small shop in the front hallway, with T-shirts, books about cats, cat toys and beds, jewelry featuring cats – whatever items they could find that celebrated cats or promoted shelter adoptions. Giving out samples during the grand opening would show how people reacted to the different options.

The woman managed to drag the kids out as they chattered with excitement. Kari would have to stop by the store tomorrow – no, she'd have to see if Marley or Mom could do it – and pick up a bunch of stickers or cheap trinkets featuring cats to make sure they had enough for any kids who showed up for the grand opening.

Maybe the café wouldn't get a huge crowd that weekend. It didn't matter. Kari now had confidence that the café could be a success, whether they opened with a bang or a murmur. People had been finding them. Customers loved the food, the coffee, and most of all the cats. Word would spread.

Tomorrow would be fine.

It was tonight that had her worried.

She freshened up in the bathroom and headed down the hall. Holly smirked and said, "Good luck" as she left. How did the barista even know Kari's plans for the evening? No secrets in the workplace, apparently.

Oh no, had Colin figured it out?

Would it be better if he had?

Kari paced up and down the hall. Marley came out of the kitchen, winked, and said good night.

Colin appeared at the far end of the hall. She'd asked him to look over their budget, both because he should know, and to get him out of the way as she cleaned and people left.

Marley turned the sign on the door to Closed and walked out.

"Isn't she staying?" Colin asked. "Or does she have to pick up Brian?"

Kari managed a nervous smile. "It's only the two of us tonight."

Colin frowned. "Oh?"

Oh no. He was disappointed. He was upset that he had to spend the evening alone with her. Her plans crumbled.

Colin's expression slowly shifted to a smile. "Okay by me."

Whew. That must have been an "I'm puzzled" frown, not an "I'm unhappy" frown.

Now if she could find her nerve. She took two steps toward him, dragging air into lungs that felt too small. "Colin."

A rap sounded on the door.

Kari jumped and gasped. She turned away to hide her embarrassment and scurried for the door.

Kari fished cash out of her pocket. Colin came up behind her and took the pizza from the delivery woman. Once the door was closed and locked, Colin said, "Pizza? Are you trying to spoil me?"

Well, yes.

"I figured we should have dinner before we get down to business." Kari winced. Really, get down to business? Thank goodness Colin did not yet know that her plans for the evening did not include work.

"Let's drag a couple of chairs and a little table out here," she said. "That way the furry thieves won't try to steal our cheese, and we don't have to wrangle them all into the back room."

He put the pizza on the counter. "I'll move the furniture if you keep the cats from escaping."

Kari held the door for Colin and shooed away cats that tried to pass. Finally, they sat down with their pizzas, and bottles of beer left over from the construction day.

Colin smiled across at her. "This is nice."

Kari nodded and managed to smile back despite her tight jaw. Would she even be able to choke down the pizza?

She took a bite and chewed slowly.

This was a bad idea. She and Colin worked together. They were business partners.

Two more bites.

She shouldn't say anything. She could find chores for them to do and pretend she really had wanted to prep for the grand opening. Even if they cleaned things that were already clean, Colin would accept that. Everyone knew her perfectionist tendencies.

She washed down her pizza with gulps of beer.

Maybe she should let their relationship follow its natural course. If things were supposed to happen, they would happen, right?

She managed a few more bites.

Maybe she should let Colin take the lead. If he was interested, he'd say something eventually, right?

The last bite made it past her throat.

Maybe, maybe, maybe.

No.

She couldn't face six more months, or even another month, of not knowing how he felt.

She cared about Colin. He deserved to know that.

He gave her a sympathetic smile. "Nervous about tomorrow?"

"Yeah." Nervous, but not about that. "That is, not really." She bit her lip and gazed at him.

He would appreciate honesty. Look how he'd noticed her nerves around his missing limb and had told her straight out that she could ask about it. She wanted that openness in a relationship.

"It's okay if you are," he said. "We'll get through it together."

Kari nodded and managed a smile.

She hadn't been fair to Marley, making plans for her sister's future without actually including her sister in those plans. It was time to stop trying to do what she thought was best for everyone else. She needed to ask what they thought was best, and then help them get that, if they wanted her help.

"You okay?"

She nodded.

It was time to decide what she wanted, and say it out loud. If Colin didn't feel the same way, then Kari would get over her feelings and they'd go back to being coworkers, business partners, and friends. That wouldn't be the end of the world.

Kari sipped more beer to ease the tightness in her throat. She had to do this now, or she'd wind up choking on her food. Colin would have to call an ambulance, and that was not the evening she had planned.

Colin finished his second slice of pizza. "You're not eating much. Let's work first and eat later. Maybe you'll feel better after we get some things done."

Kari let out a weak laugh. Exactly what she'd been thinking. Except not at all the same thing. "Right. Sure."

"How about a little sugar boost first?" He offered her the plate that had been sitting on the counter. "I see Marley didn't put away all the baked goods. I'm assuming that's intentional, for us."

Yes, good. She could clear the taste of pizza and beer from her mouth. She chose a lemon bar and nibbled at it. Colin took an espresso brownie.

A few minutes later, he rose. "Ready?" He gave her shoulder a gentle squeeze, and headed for the main room.

Kari wiped her damp hands on a napkin and followed.

Colin stopped in the middle of the room and looked around. "The place looks great. What did you want to do? Make more posters for tomorrow? Should we bring out the prize boxes already? We don't want cats to get into them."

Cleopatra jumped down from the bench and trotted up to Colin, mewing. She rubbed her face against his boots.

He sat on the floor and petted her. "Yes, I know, you love my boots. I wonder if it's this pair in particular, or any leather boots. Should I give her these and get new ones for myself?"

Kari crouched beside them. "I have to think it's at least partly the man inside the boots. I haven't seen her like this with anyone else."

"I guess we'll find out when I take her home and take my boots off." He gave a quick sideways glance at Kari. "I wonder how she'll feel about the prostheses."

"She's a sensible lady. She won't care."

Actually, it would be interesting to see if the cats reacted at all to the prostheses, and if they treated the one that looked like a leg differently from the other one. Kari had no idea what the cats would think, but she hoped

Colin would get the message behind her statement. What he'd suffered, what he'd overcome, simply made him the incredible man he was.

He wasn't missing anything. He was everything.

He looked down at the cat, but Kari thought his smile might be for her.

"You do think she and Samson will get along, right?" he asked.

"They're a perfect pair, and you're perfect for them. The only question might be, can you fit both of them in your lap. They're not our smallest cats."

He laughed. "Maybe I should test it."

"Sure. Find a seat. Samson was in that hammock a minute ago. I'll get him." Colin might have been joking about testing it now, but this gave Kari something to do, a way to delay for a few more seconds. Plus, having two cats in his lap would surely put Colin in an agreeable mood.

She scooped Samson out of his hammock. They asked customers not to pick up the cats, because people might lift them the wrong way, or some cats might not like being held. But Kari knew this sweet boy didn't mind.

She carried him to the bench as Colin settled down with Cleopatra.

Samson gave a mew of greeting as Kari put him down. He batted at Cleopatra a few times, but when she didn't respond, he settled down along Colin's thigh and purred.

Colin rested his hand and forearm along the cat. "Maybe not quite room in the lap, but they'll manage."

Kari stroked her hand over Samson. The edge of her little finger brushed Colin's hand.

Her gaze down, she said, "If you ever want an extra lap, I'll volunteer mine."

Colin didn't answer right away. Finally she raised her gaze to his.

"I'd like that," he said. "It's funny that you've never seen my place. I feel like I know your family so well, but then I remember it's only been a few weeks. I don't have anywhere near the history of you and Adam."

"Yeah, but ..." She looked away. She couldn't figure out what to do with her hands. "You still feel like part of the family. Not like Adam, though." She glanced back at him.

His lips pressed together and turned down.

Kari went on. "He's like a brother. You're ..." She licked her lips. "Not."

His lips twitched upward. She wanted to press hers to them.

"What exactly am I like?" he asked. "Something good, I hope."

She swallowed and forced herself to meet his gaze. "So good. Like ..."

His growing smile gave Kari the courage to continue.

"You're like rocky road fudge bars, full of good things. You're like espresso brownies right out of the oven. Warm and gooey – not literally, you know what I mean – and comforting and sweet, with exactly the right kick of excitement."

He was grinning now, his body shaking in silent laughter. Cleopatra grumbled and shifted on his lap.

Kari placed her hand on top of Colin's. Why had she been so afraid? She was speaking the truth, and that made it easy. "In case I'm being too subtle, what I'm trying to say is I'm falling for you. Or maybe I've already fallen."

He turned his hand over and laced his fingers with hers. "Maybe you would have understood my lemon bar metaphor after all."

"Your ... what?"

"Something I thought of awhile back. Actually, it was the day we first met Samson, when I ran from him." He looked down and used his pinky finger to give Samson's jaw a quick rub while leaving his other fingers entwined with Kari's.

The Siamese shifted to his back and wrapped his front paws around Colin and Kari's wrists.

Colin said, "You're like a lemon bar, the perfect mix of sweet and tart."

"Oh, right. I remember something like that. Marley was, what, a blondie?"

"I think so, but we're not talking about her."

"We're talking about me, the lemon bar." Kari thought for a minute and nodded. "I like it. It is a compliment. I think that's one of the things I like best about you. You see me. I know I'm not perfect, even if I'm a perfectionist. I think I know what's best for everyone and I tend to manipulate people. I'm trying to stop that. I'll do better, I promise, and you can help by letting me know when I'm doing it."

"Sure, although you are cute when you're in charge. I don't mean that in a condescending way. I adore seeing you take on people who might think you don't know what you're doing because you're young and female. You get tough and smart, and it's sexy as all get-out. But when you're trying to control your family or friends, I'll say something."

"I can't promise I won't get annoyed at first, when you call me on it. I will try to accept it eventually." Kari pressed her shoulder against his. "I also like the way you take everything in stride. It helps me feel calmer simply to be around you."

He squeezed her hand. "Then I'd better spend a lot of time around you."

She clung to his hand and looked into his eyes. "Does this mean … you know how I feel, right? That I'm crazy about you? Does this mean you want to, well, date?"

She rubbed her free hand over her face. "I feel like we're in grade school again. I should've given you one of those notes with a box to check if you like me. This is why I don't tell people how I feel."

He was laughing again. "It's all right, I'm glad we're talking about this. I've been thinking about it for a long time."

"You have?"

"I liked you right away, but I wasn't sure if I was ready for a relationship. Same as I wasn't sure if I was ready for one cat, let alone two."

He tried to move their joined hands toward Cleopatra, but Samson dragged their wrists back to himself.

"See," Colin said, "cats know how to ask for what they want. He wants more pets, so he's demanding them. When he's done, I suppose he'll bite at us. At least we don't have to wonder what he wants."

"Yeah, being clear does have some advantages." She leaned closer and gazed into his eyes. "I like you. I want to date you. I think ... I think I'm already falling in love with you. There, now you know. No more hiding."

He released her hand and managed to withdraw his arm from Samson's embrace. He turned toward her and bracketed her face with his hands. "I like you too. I want to date you. And yes, I'm falling for you, fast and hard."

They leaned in. Their lips brushed, retreated, brushed again. He tasted of chocolate with a hint of coffee. She tasted of lemons.

Together, they were unexpected, but perfect.

Dear Readers,

I hope you've enjoyed getting to know Kari and Colin. You'll see Colin and Kari together in future books in the series. For Marley's path to romance, read book 2, *Kittens and Kisses at the Cat Café*.

If you enjoyed these adventures, please leave a review on GoodReads, BookBub, Amazon or elsewhere. Reviews help authors find an audience, and they help readers find great books.

I hope you'll check out my other books. To learn more, please visit my website at www.krisbock.com or sign up for the Kris Bock newsletter at sendfox.com/KrisBock. Newsletter subscribers get a free 10,000-word story set in the world of the Furrever Friends cat café, plus printable copies of the recipes mentioned in the cat café novels.

Read on to see the recipe for the Cookie Dough Brownies mentioned in this story and then for a preview of *The Billionaire Cowboy's Christmas*.

Kris Bock

Two-For-One Cookie Dough Brownies

Dense, chewy chocolate brownies are so good. But chocolate chip cookies are amazing too. How do you decide which to make? With this recipe, you don't need to choose! A rich brownie layer is topped with raw chocolate chip cookie dough.

Note: to save a step, use your favorite packaged brownie mix for the first layer.

Ingredients for the Brownie Layer
4 large eggs
1 1/4 cups unsweetened cocoa powder
1 teaspoon salt
1 teaspoon baking powder
1 tablespoon vanilla extract
1 cup butter
2 1/4 cups sugar
1 1/2 cups flour

Cookie Dough Layer
1/2 cup butter, softened
1/4 cup sugar
1/2 cup packed brown sugar
3 tablespoons milk (or milk alternative)
1 teaspoon vanilla extract
1 cup flour
1 cup chocolate chips

Supplies
9 x 13-inch baking pan
mixing bowls
measuring cups and measuring spoons
electric mixer
wire cooling rack

1. Preheat the oven to 350 degrees. Lightly grease the baking pan.
2. In a mixing bowl, lightly beat the eggs. Add the cocoa, salt, baking powder, and vanilla. Beat at medium speed for about 1 minute, until smooth.
3. In a medium-sized microwave-safe bowl, melt the butter. Add the sugar and stir to combine.
4. Add the butter and sugar mixture to the other ingredients and stir to combine. Blend in the flour.
5. Pour the batter into the baking pan. Bake for 28 to 32 minutes. Use a cake tester or toothpick inserted into the center to test doneness. It should come out clean, or with only a few moist crumbs clinging to it. Cool the brownies in their pan on a rack.
6. Make the cookie dough layer. Cream the butter and both sugars in a mixing bowl. Blend in the milk and vanilla. Blend in the flour. Stir in the chocolate chips.
7. Drop blobs of cookie dough over the cooled brownies. Spread the cookie dough layer evenly. Cut the brownies into squares or bars and store them in the refrigerator in an airtight container.

Tip: In rare cases, raw eggs can lead to food poisoning. Therefore, food safety experts suggest you don't eat raw cookie dough. (Some of us do it anyway.) Here, the cookie dough layer does not contain eggs.

Sign up for the Kris Bock newsletter at sendfox.com/KrisBock to get a printable copy of this recipe and the rest of the recipes mentioned in this book and future cat café novels.

Keep going for a preview of *The Billionaire Cowboy's Christmas*. In the Accidental Billionaire Cowboys series, a Texas ranching family wins a billion-dollar lottery. They're advised to go into hiding, but they have animals needing care. They'll have to stay and fend off envious friends, scammers, and fortune hunters. Can they build new dreams and find love amidst the chaos?

Readers say: "Kris has a winning series here."
"All of these books have been marvelous."
"This has been one of my favorite cowboy series to read as it is so unexpected."

Excerpt: The Billionaire Cowboy's Christmas by Kris Bock Chapter 1

Josh Tomlinson paused on the porch to shake water from his jacket and stomp the mud off his boots. He couldn't complain about rain in Texas. The grass needed it, and they needed grass to feed the livestock. But rain reminded him that the barn roof needed repairs. They also had to tear up the old cement slab that was rotting, level the ground, and pour a new slab. Even if he and his brothers did the labor themselves, they were looking at ten thousand dollars in materials. So yeah, rain wasn't his favorite thing right now.

Plus, some folks claimed a wet November meant a snowy December. What if they had another winter with those heavy snows and weeks of below freezing temperatures? Sure, snow was pretty, when you didn't have to work in it, with frozen hands and wind cutting through your jacket and trying to steal your hat, and when you didn't have to worry about how you were going to pay the heating bill and keep your family and all your animals alive and healthy.

Okay, maybe he could complain about the rain.

He stepped inside, hung up his jacket, and left his boots under the bench inside the front door. His mama sat at the big table in the main room straight ahead. To his right, the sofa faced the TV and formed the divider between the dining room and living room. His brother TC lounged on one end with his feet up, so he could see their mama at the table behind the sofa. Their youngest brother, Xander, sat on the other end with his laptop on his knees.

"Josh!" Mama looked up with a smile. "Come get warm."

He bent to kiss her cheek. They had their money troubles, being rich in land but poor in cash, like a lot of ranchers. But they were still here, at least most of them. Some of the tension left his shoulders as heat warmed his chilled skin.

"We're planning what we'll do when we win the lottery," TC said.

Josh merely grunted and went into the kitchen. Something simmered in the crockpot, giving off savory smells, but Josh headed for the coffeepot. It would be decaf this time of day, but it would warm him up. He filled his mug and went back to the table, sitting catty-corner from his mother.

"Come on, Xander," TC said. "You can come up with something better than that."

Xander didn't look up from his computer screen. "All I really need is a new computer."

"But we're talking a billion dollars!" TC said. "You could buy, like, a million computers."

"A billion is one thousand million. I could build a good computer for one thousand dollars, but it's more like thirty-five hundred for an excellent business computer. Call it four thousand dollars with software. So, I could buy a quarter of a million computers. But I only need one." Xander frowned for a few seconds. "Although it would be handy to have a full backup system in case something breaks."

Josh chuckled. Xander had earned the nickname the Professor when he graduated high school at fifteen. He'd been helping with the ranch's accounting since age twelve, annoying their father by finding math errors, until finally Daddy had handed over the financial records to Xander entirely. Thank goodness for that. Daddy had died when Josh, the oldest son, was only twenty-four. Josh had his hands full supporting Mama and trying to keep the ranch running. At least he could trust Xander with the numbers.

TC did his share of the work but always had some crazy idea about how to make the ranch pay better. And Cody had taken off the minute he could, even before Daddy died.

"Why are we talking about billions of dollars anyway?" Josh asked.

Xander twisted around to look at him. "Only one billion."

"Oh, is that all?"

"What would you do with that kind of money, Josh?" TC asked.

"I don't know." Josh didn't see the point of thinking about impossibilities. "I suppose you'd buy your ostriches, or was it emus?"

"I would absolutely buy a herd of ostriches. Maybe emus as well. Also llamas, for the wool."

"I don't think ostriches are very friendly," Xander said.

"Good meat though," TC said. "The average wholesale price is twenty dollars a pound."

"You only make about fifteen hundred dollars per bird," Xander said. "You get almost twice that per cow."

"Well, sure, a cow weighs four times as much as an ostrich," TC said. "It also takes more land and water."

Josh merely shook his head. TC wanted to expand from cattle farming. He called it diversifying and exploring new markets. Josh called it taking unnecessary risks. Josh had already agreed to the small herd of bison, and so far, that experiment was doing fine, but TC had all these big ideas and wanted to do them all now. At least Xander backed up Josh when it came to the financial discussions. They simply couldn't risk money on experiments, not when they had so many other financial obligations.

"Why are we talking about money we don't have?" Josh asked.

"Lottery," TC and Xander said together.

Josh turned to his mother. "Right, your knitting group met today. But if you'd won the lottery, I'd have heard about it already."

Mama held up one more ticket. "The group didn't win, but I bought an extra ticket for the family, since the amount is so high."

"You know that doesn't improve your odds," Xander said. "Anyway, the winner—assuming there is one this week—won't get that much all at once. The billion could be split among multiple winners, and then you have taxes."

A billion dollars? Josh's mind boggled. He could barely conceive of a tenth of that, a hundredth of that. Ten thousand dollars would take care of the ranch's immediate needs. One hundred thousand would let them make important improvements and keep some money in the bank for the future. People used phrases like a billion dollars when talking about the federal government's budget, not the finances of ordinary folks.

What about a million? He could almost grasp the idea of having that in the bank, since he knew a few people who were millionaires even without counting the value of their ranches. A million dollars must feel warm and comforting, like a thick blanket covering you up at the end of a long day when you'd finally, finally ticked everything off the to-do list. With that much, he could take care of the ranch, take care of Mama, give Xander his computers, and let TC play around with his giant birds.

But why would anyone need more than a million dollars, let alone a thousand million dollars?

"You know you're dreaming about things that will never happen." Josh reached over to squeeze his mother's hand to take the sting out of the words.

She laughed. "Oh, sweetie, I don't expect to win. But for a few minutes, we all get to dream."

Josh didn't have an answer for that. Buying lottery tickets seemed like a waste of money to him. Weren't you more likely to get hit by lightning? And you didn't have to pay for that privilege. But he so rarely saw his mother laugh these days. Not since Daddy died eight years ago. When they were growing up, Mama had been full of laughter, always ready to join in their games or giggle at a prank, so long as no one got hurt. She hadn't expected to be widowed at age fifty.

Josh hadn't expected to be the man of the house at twenty-four either. But they'd managed. Holding on by the fingernails sometimes, but they hadn't lost the ranch.

So, okay, Mama could have her dreams.

"What would you buy with the money then?" Josh asked her. "If you became a billionaire."

She laughed again. "You mean if we became billionaires. You'd each get your share."

"Gosh, thanks." He had to smile at the idea of sharing their imaginary money. "But what about you? What would you want?"

She so rarely asked for anything. She hadn't even hinted at what she might like for Christmas. If she gave them some idea, and if they could make it happen . . . Something small enough . . .

"Oh, I don't know." She spread her hands. "Travel? See the world? I've never been outside of Texas."

Nothing he could buy her. Well, maybe a trip across the border, down to Mexico? Xander could go with her. TC and Josh couldn't leave the ranch unless they hired people to do the work in their absence, and they certainly couldn't afford that.

"Maybe I'd buy my own house, leave you boys the ranch," she mused. "Not too far away though, so I could see you every day, you and someday your wives and children."

"Sorry, Mama, I don't think you can buy us wives and children," TC said.

"Being rich wouldn't hurt your chances any," Mama said. "I can't believe I have two boys over thirty, and two in their twenties, and none of you even have a girlfriend—at least that you've told me!"

"Hey, I'm barely thirty," TC said. "Nag Josh. He's the old man."

Yeah, right, like he could afford a wife and kids.

"I don't know why you play the lottery if you want things money can't buy." Josh smiled at his mother, but his heart hurt. As the only woman living with three grown men—four when Cody visited—no wonder she wished for a daughter-in-law or two. She wasn't old, far from it, with plenty of brown amongst the gray in her hair, but with Daddy gone so early, she might wonder if she'd live long enough to see grandchildren.

But who had time for dating? His brothers, maybe, but not Josh. Anyway, he had enough people depending on him. He didn't need someone else to worry about, when he had three brothers and his mother to support. Well, Cody took care of himself. He'd gotten his pilot's license and now worked as a crop duster, but he might come back someday. That would make Mama happy, but all four brothers living together might cause the house to explode.

"I could buy a mansion." She nodded. "Lots of rooms, so you could all come and stay with me. And I'd pay someone else to clean it!"

Maybe they could hire someone to clean the house as her Christmas present? Not all the time, but at least once.

"Okay, fine," Josh said. "Now we know what we'd do if we won all that money. You'd get a big house, Xander would get computers, and TC would get his big birds—penguins, was it?"

TC cackled. "Oh, I'd totally get penguins if I was a billionaire!"

"That's a comic book villain move," Xander said. "Plus, penguins might not do well in Texas."

"Cody would probably buy another plane," Josh said. "A private jet maybe."

"And you?" Mama would not leave that alone.

"I don't know. I'd fix up the ranch first thing. After that . . . it's hard to imagine."

"Oh, sweetie." She took his hand and squeezed. "You had too much responsibility too young. That's why you forgot how to dream."

What did one say to that?

He scrambled for an answer. "I can dream! I'd, um, put in a swimming pool."

He absolutely would not. What would be the point? It was one more thing to take care of, and he got enough exercise working all day. But it was the first thing that popped into his head, something that people with money and free time had.

"Okay, where is this extra ticket? Let's find out how much we won." He really meant, let's put this conversation behind us and eat dinner. The coffee had warmed him up some, but he still felt chilled in his bones, and hungry, and worn out. A lottery ticket wasn't going to fix any of that.

"All right." Mama rummaged through her purse and came up with a card that looked kind of like a receipt. "Xander, you want to bring up the numbers, honey?"

"On it." He tapped his computer.

"Didn't you already check the knitting group's numbers?" Josh asked.

Mama giggled, still giddy with the fun of merely imagining something good happening. "You know I'm not one for numbers. I bought five tickets for the group and we each looked at one when they first read off the numbers. I just scanned for each number. Didn't get a single one!"

Josh leaned forward to look at the lottery ticket. He hadn't paid much attention to them before. It looked like the ticket had six numbers of one or two digits. "You have to get all of those to win?"

"You only have to get one number to win two dollars," Mama said. "We've done that sometimes. We even won ten dollars once."

After paying two dollars per ticket, and buying five tickets each week for the knitting group. Well, it was cheaper than cigarettes, and healthier to boot.

"You have a one in twenty-four chance of winning a prize." Xander was reading from the website. "To win the jackpot, you have to get all six numbers. Your chances are less than one in three hundred million."

"Oh, is that all? Well, come on!" Josh waved his hand. "Let's do it."

"Okay. Ready?" Xander read off a number and paused.

Mama gasped. "We got that one!" She made a tiny tick mark below the number.

Hooray, they'd win back the price of the ticket. But Mama got a few more seconds of joy, so it was worth it.

Xander read off the next number.

Mama scanned the ticket. "We got that one too!"

Josh leaned over. She might have made a mistake.

Nope, they really did have two of the numbers. Not bad.

Xander read the third number.

Mama stared at the ticket. She angled it so Josh could see, her finger below another number. He studied it and looked up to meet her wide eyes. He nodded.

TC and Xander were both looking over the back of the couch at them. "Well?" TC asked.

Mama nodded rapidly with her lips pressed together.

"Yeah," Josh croaked. Okay, he could see how people got caught up in this.

"Hang on, that's—" Xander studied the computer screen. His shoulders slumped. "Only ten dollars."

Josh met his mother's eyes and they both chuckled. Silly, getting so excited over ten dollars. But it wasn't the numbers they'd already matched that did it; it was the thought that maybe they'd match another one. It gave you hope, which would then come crashing down, so you'd chase that hope again and again. This must be how people got addicted to gambling. But gambling didn't pay off: the house always came out ahead. In a few minutes it would be over, and they'd be back to reality with all its struggles.

"Okay, next number." Xander read it out loud. He and TC twisted around again.

Mama put her hand over her mouth. She slid the ticket to Josh again.

He peered at it. "What? No way!"

"What?" TC demanded.

"We're doing something wrong," Josh said. "Let me read the numbers to you." He read back the first four numbers.

Xander was now kneeling on the couch with his laptop propped on the back of it. "Those are correct. We won five hundred dollars!"

They all grinned at each other. Part of Josh's mind was already thinking about how they should spend the money. They had things they needed, but Christmas was coming up, and if it was free money, maybe they could send Mama and Xander to Mexico for a few days. Hotel, food, a few souvenirs. Five hundred dollars would cover a long weekend, right?

Mama took a deep breath and blew it out. "Okay. Wow. This is exciting. I know we're not—I'm sure that's it, but—oh, let's finish up with the last numbers and then figure out how to collect our five hundred dollars."

Josh pushed the ticket back toward her, but she shook her head. "You do it. I'm afraid I'll get too excited and read it wrong."

He shrugged and nodded at Xander to continue. Xander read the fifth number.

Josh swallowed. He couldn't take his eyes off the ticket. "How much do you win with five numbers?" His voice sounded far away.

"Those five numbers would be one million dollars," Xander said.

"No way. You have to be pranking us." TC swung himself over the back of the couch. Mama didn't even notice, her gaze intent on Josh, too distracted to scold.

Josh carefully turned the ticket around so TC could read it. He flinched when TC grabbed the ticket. "Careful!"

"I'm not gonna—holy guacamole with extra hot sauce. We won a million dollars!" TC swung around and leaned over Xander's shoulder. "Look, it's true! We got five numbers!"

Xander looked at the ticket. At his computer screen. Back at the ticket. They all held their breath. Xander would know if they'd made a mistake, if they'd mixed up the numbers somehow. Josh waited for the disappointment, the correction that no, it was a mix-up, they were back at five hundred dollars or maybe only ten. Even five hundred would seem disappointing now, when it was so exciting seconds ago.

"We didn't win one million dollars," Xander said.

The excitement dropped away so fast Josh felt like he'd slide out of his chair. It figured. So much for dreams. So much for hope. They didn't get you anywhere. Nothing but hard work did.

Xander put his computer carefully on the coffee table, stood up, and turned around. "We got all six numbers. We won the jackpot. We're billionaires."

Read on to learn more about Kris's novels.

About the Author

Kris Bock is the author of romantic suspense novels, the Accidental Detective humorous mystery series, the Accidental Billionaire Cowboys sweet romance series, the Felony Melanie: Sweet Home Alabama romantic comedy novels, and the Furrever Friends cat cafe sweet romance series.

Learn more at www.krisbock.com. Sign up for Kris Bock newsletter at sendfox.com/KrisBock for announcements of new books, sales, and more. Newsletter subscribers get a free 10,000-word story set in the world of the Furrever Friends cat café, printable copies of the recipes mentioned in the cat café novels, and a short story from the Accidental Detective humorous mystery series.

The Furrever Friends Sweet Romance series features the workers and customers at a small-town cat café, and the adorable cats and kittens looking for their forever homes. Each book is a complete story with a happy ending for one couple (and maybe more than one rescued cat).

Kittens and Kisses at the Cat Café – book 2

He's loved her forever. She still sees him as the neighbor kid. Can five desperate kittens bring them together?
"I absolutely loved this book! I can't wait to read more about these wonderful people!"

Tea and Temptation at the Cat Café – book 3

Can two lonely people carrying scars from the past get a second chance at finding love?
"A fun and easy read, perfect for relaxing and getting away from it all."

Romance and Rescues at the Cat Café – book 4

Can getting stranded in a creepy house full of abandoned cats turn these enemies into friends—or even something more?
"The Cat Café characters—especially the cat characters!—are so much fun."

Christmas Cookies at the Cat Café – book 5

Christmas isn't the same since Diane's kids grew up and her husband died – so when her high school sweetheart comes back to town, maybe it's time for some cozy new holiday traditions.
"It's a perfect book to snuggle up with during the holiday season."

Cupcakes and Confessions at The Cat Café – book 6

Fiona gave up her baby for adoption 23 years ago. When Sean notes how much she looks like his coworker, Fiona is suddenly reunited with her grown-up daughter. Sean steadies Fiona through this emotional roller coaster, but she doesn't have room for romance – does she?
"This is a beautifully written story about love, connecting with family, small towns, friends, and adorable cats."

In **the Accidental Billionaire Cowboys series**, a Texas ranching family wins a billion-dollar lottery. They're advised to go into hiding, but they have animals needing care. They'll have to stay and fend off envious friends, scammers, and fortune hunters. Can they build new dreams and find love amidst the chaos?

The Billionaire Cowboy's Christmas
Charming the Billionaire Cowboy
The Billionaire Cowboy's Proposition
The Billionaire Cowgirl's Christmas
The Billionaire Cowgirl's Christmas

Readers say: "All of these books have been marvelous."
"I was hooked from the start. This book series just keeps getting better."
"Kris has created a beautiful family with special significant others. I highly recommend this book and series."

Big City, Big Glamour, Big Trouble

Check out the new series featuring "Felony Melanie" a decade before the events of the movie *Sweet Home Alabama*.

Kris writes a series with her brother, scriptwriter Douglas J Eboch, who wrote the original screenplay for the movie *Sweet Home Alabama*. Follow the crazy antics of Melanie, Jake, and their friends a decade before the events of the movie.

Sign up for our Rom-Com newsletter at sendfox.com/lp/1rpny3 and get "Felony Melanie Destroys the Moonshiner's Cabin." These first two chapters from the novel *Felony Melanie in Pageant Pandemonium* stand alone as a short story. In the future, you'll get fun content about upcoming Felony Melanie novels and other romantic comedy news and links. Or find the series at all major book retailers.

Felony Melanie in Pageant Pandemonium
Felony Melanie in the Big Smashup
Felony Melanie and the Prank War

Head back in time to the early 1990s for this laugh out loud rom com based on one of the best rom com movies of all time. Readers love the series: "Laugh out loud funny with high school hi-jinx."

"If you liked the movie Sweet Home Alabama, you'll love the books that tell the stories leading up to the movie."

"Fun loving, laugh out loud read!!!!"

> A witty journalist solves mysteries in Arizona and tackles the challenges of turning fifty.
>
> Book Reviews: "A great start to a new series." "a fast-paced book that keeps you thinking." "grabbed me from the first page to the last."

In the **Accidental Detective humorous mystery series**, a witty journalist solves mysteries in Arizona and tackles the challenges of turning fifty.

Book 1 is *Something Shady at Sunshine Haven*: When patients are dying at an Alzheimer's unit, a former war correspondent must use her journalism skills to uncover the killer and save her mother. Kate has followed the most dangerous news stories around the world, but can she survive going home?

Something Shady at Sunshine Haven
Something Deadly on Desert Drive
Someone Cruel in Coyote Creek
Someone Missing from Malapais Mountain
Someone Murderous at The Midnight Motel
Someone Rotten Riding the Rails

Readers say: "This series is so enjoyable to read and funny too. If you enjoy suspense, mystery and a little romance along with a lotta laughs, you will enjoy this book."
"This is a terrific series and I enjoy both the mystery storyline as well as the characters and their interactions."

Kris also writes romantic suspense with outdoor adventures and Southwestern landscapes, called "Smart romance with an 'Indiana Jones' feel." *Desert Gold* follows the hunt for a long-lost treasure in the New Mexico desert. In *Valley of Gems*, estranged relatives compete to reach a buried treasure by following a series of complex clues. In *Silver Canyon*, sparks fly when reader favorites Camie and Tiger help a mysterious man track down his missing uncle.

Whispers in the Dark features archaeology and intrigue among ancient Southwest ruins. *What We Found* is a mystery with strong romantic elements about a young woman who finds a murder victim in the woods. In *Counterfeits*, stolen Rembrandt paintings bring danger to a small New Mexico town.

Pig River Press
Socorro, New Mexico
Copyright © 2019 Christine Eboch

All rights reserved. For information about permission to reproduce selections from this book, contact the author through her website at www.krisbock.com.

This is a work of fiction. Names, characters, places, and incidents other than historical references are the product of the author's imagination. Any resemblance to actual persons, living or dead, is entirely coincidental.

Made in the USA
Middletown, DE
11 December 2024